DARK SHADOWS

A GIA SANTELLA CRIME THRILLER
BOOK 11

KRISTI BELCAMINO

LIQUID MIND PUBLISHING

Liquid Mind Publishing

Special thanks to Robin Paradis-Kent for her keen typo-hunting eye.
Anything that slipped past after her perusal is my fault entirely.

GIA SANTELLA CRIME THRILLER SERIES

Enjoying the Gia Santella series? Scan below to order more books today!

Vendetta

Vigilante

Vengeance

Black Widow

Day of the Dead

Border Line

Night Fall

Stone Cold

Cold as Death

Cold Blooded

Dark Shadows

Dark Vengeance

Dark Justice

Deadly Justice

Deadly Lies

1

WHEN NICO AND I FIRST LOOKED AT APARTMENTS IN BARCELONA, we didn't have strong ideas about what we wanted other than it be located in the Gothic Quarter. The quarter was central to everything. It was near the beach and the main pedestrian artery of the city, Las Ramblas, and it overflowed with character. Below our balcony, the narrow street was filled with small mom-and-pop shops that had everything we could possibly desire—cheese, wine, bread. You know, the basic necessities.

But when we walked into this apartment, besides its gorgeous architecture, what I fell in love with was the alcove that was specifically designated as an ofrenda—a home altar for those you loved who had died. Even though I'm Italian and it's a Mexican tradition, it spoke to me on the deepest level of my soul.

Although some people only set up ofrendas around Dia de los Muertos, mine was in place all year long.

Now, as I wheeled my gunmetal gray suitcase over to the front door, I glanced at the altar. I would miss it the most. I wasn't sure when I'd be back in Barcelona. If ever.

The ofrenda was set in a deep oval alcove in the wall that contained photos, candles, and mementos from those I'd loved the most in this life: my parents, Bobby—my first true love, and Nico—my last true love.

Nico wasn't dead, but his picture was there along with all the other people I'd loved and lost in my life.

Was that sacrilegious? Fuck if I knew.

But the truth was the Nico I'd known and loved was dead.

Alzheimer's had taken him from me. He didn't know me anymore. Now, I was just some girl he groped when I showed up. At first it had broken my heart. But once I realized that the Nico I'd known and loved was no longer there, in some ways it'd been easier to let go.

I stared at the photos. The photo of my parents was one of them smiling on a boat, their hair windblown. My mother held a glass of wine. My father had his arm around her.

I missed my parents so much. I'd been robbed of them before I was barely old enough to drink. They had been my whole world.

The photo of Bobby was a snapshot I'd taken of him in Italy. He'd been standing on our balcony looking out at the sea. He was so damn handsome. That was the day I'd finally told him I loved him. Within 24 hours he'd be dead. The son of my parents' killer took him away.

A tear slipped down my cheek as I looked at the photo of Nico.

He looked like a sophisticated movie star and a powerful leader. Which is what he had been. My greatest love. The man I had intended to spend the rest of my life with. That man had loved me more than any woman could dream of being loved, but he had been taken away from me slowly and cruelly by the creeping dementia that stole his memories and light.

When I realized that Nico was gone, I decided to never allow myself to fall in love again.

It hurt too much. Why would I fucking torture myself like that again? Who in their right mind would do that? Um...nobody.

I was fucking done.

There is an old Italian saying that we only truly love three people in our lives.

I've loved my three.

Bobby. Nico. James.

Dear, sweet James who, thank God, was still alive and thriving in San Francisco. That man had stolen my heart but then broke it into a million pieces. Because I'm a killer and he was a cop. Our relationship never stood a chance.

I reached into my bag and took out my worn metal Zippo lighter and lit the candles on my ofrenda one last time.

I lit four of them. Along with the photos and candles, I'd placed mementos that reminded me of them or items that they had loved in life.

In front of Nico's picture, I'd placed a CD of his favorite music and a bottle of tequila.

For Bobby, a bottle of the hot sauce he loved and his favorite book of poetry.

For my parents, the cigars my dad liked and the perfume my mom wore.

My phone vibrated in my bag, startling me out of my memories.

I rummaged around and found it just as the call ended. Dante.

I called him back. "Yo."

"I've been buzzing. I'm downstairs."

"Oh, fuck. The ringer is still broken. I'll buzz you in."

I hit the button and headed back to the bedroom to finish packing my second suitcase.

Soon Dante was at my side.

"Have you decided where you're going?" he said in his perfectly enunciated speech as he walked in.

I glanced up at him and was once again astonished by his good looks. The guy never aged. We'd been friends since we were kids, and he just kept getting better looking. His brilliant white smile always stood out against his burnished olive skin, and I loved how he was wearing his silky black hair a little bit long in the back nowadays at the request of his husband, Wayne. Today, he was wearing a white linen shirt with the buttons undone enough for me to see his gold necklace with the Italian cornetto and hand talisman to protect against the evil eye.

"French Riviera," I said.

I continued throwing expensive silk lingerie into my smaller suitcase. Dante had made me buy it during our last shopping spree in Paris. I would never have spent $250 on underwear otherwise, but I had to admit it made my ass look spectacular.

"Sounds fabulous," Dante said, stepping into my closet. "Why there?"

"I have no memories there."

"What? That hurts. Me. You. St. Tropez?" he started humming some song about St. Tropez and dancing around.

"I'm not going there."

"Where to, then?"

I didn't answer, but I looked pointedly at a framed poster in the hallway. It was a still from the movie *La Piscine*. The movie was set in Italy. But from the look on Dante's face, I knew he made the connection. Cannes was the film epicenter of Southern France, and the festival was next week.

"Oh. My. God."

I hid my smile.

"What will you wear?"

"I'm going to sunbathe and read and listen to music and maybe find some hot boy to fuck."

Dante stopped dancing.

I could feel his disapproval without looking at him.

"You're married."

"Am I?"

He didn't answer.

I wasn't married. Not really.

How could I be? Nico didn't know who I was. He hadn't for months.

"At least let me dress you." Dante had personal buyers at all the top designers and attended the fashion shows in Paris every year. He had impeccable taste. Thank God one of us did.

"I'm bringing every bikini I own," I said. "That's really all I plan on needing."

"Darling, if you are going to be in Cannes during the Film Festival—first, how the holy hell did you find a place to stay there right now? Oh, never mind, you're Gia. But please, please tell me you'll let me dress you for the festival."

I shrugged and tossed another bikini into the suitcase on the bed.

"I wasn't planning on going to the festival."

"I'm going to get you tickets."

I didn't argue. I loved movies. Attending the festival in Cannes could fit into my hedonistic plans. "Sure. Whatever."

"Then it's a deal. Now, what should you wear? I'm not sure you have anything in this apartment?" He started thumbing through my hangers.

"I'll find something."

"I'll handle it," he said firmly. "Someone has to stop you from wearing your beat-up leather pants and 'Fuck Authority' T-shirt."

"Rosie took that shirt from me years ago."

Rosie was Nico's daughter. The closest thing I had to a child. She was off somewhere killing someone. Because, apparently, that's what the women in my family did. We couldn't help it. But there were always evil fuckers who needed to be killed.

"Will you let me do what I do best?" Dante said, in seventh heaven. Shopping and dressing me was his favorite thing ever. Or at least that's how it seemed.

"Yeah. I'll go watch some movies. And you can dress me for them."

Dante was chattering on and on about how he knew the perfect dress for me and that he might have to order it and have it sent to me in Cannes. But I would also need three other ones and…blah blah blah. I let him ramble. It made him happy so I tolerated it. And the simple fact was that I looked like shit when I dressed myself.

Attending the Cannes Film Festival was probably a legit reason to dress up.

Dante frowned. "There is nothing here. Nothing at all. Come with me," he said and grabbed my hand. "There is one place in town—one place in all of Barcelona—that might possibly have a dress that will do in a pinch if I can't get the dresses I have in mind ordered in time."

I couldn't help but laugh. God love Dante.

I grabbed my bag and followed him out the door, giving one last glance at the candles burning on the altar. I usually was very careful about blowing them out before I left the apartment, but I was feeling careless, reckless, and a small part of me thought that burning the place down would be apropos—leaving the charred remains of my life behind. But then I remembered other people lived in the building and leaned over to blow them out.

Then I steeled myself for some hard-core shopping. I wished I had some marijuana but would have to shop stone-cold sober.

But if I was being honest with myself, I was happy to spend another few hours with Dante.

He had flown into Barcelona from San Diego when he heard I was taking off for a few months...or forever.

It would be strange to leave Nico behind and not visit him daily while hoping there might be a glimmer of recognition in his eyes when he saw me.

There never was.

Nico was in good hands. I paid a small fortune every month for the memory care center to treat him like a king. It took about six months of him not recognizing me for me to realize my daily, doting presence there was no longer for him, only for me. And that it hurt like hell to be around him.

I was a coward.

I was going to leave him. Maybe forever.

If I thought there was the slightest, smallest part of him that still remembered me, I would stay. But there wasn't.

My heart was shattered.

Every morning I woke and lay in bed waiting for the dark shadows to recede from my nightmares only to realize that it wasn't a bad dream. It was my life.

Finally, I realized I had to leave Barcelona. At first I wanted to buy a house in the mountains somewhere and live like a recluse. There was still a chance I might. But right then, all my body craved was sunshine.

I'd spent the past few years as a caregiver, taking care of Nico, trying to glimpse fragments of who he used to be before he became angry and confused.

We rarely stepped outside unless it was to take him out to the garden for a walk. But now he refused to do even that.

I needed to lay in the sun and do things that weren't good for me so I didn't have to feel or think anymore.

Cannes would be the backdrop for my debauchery.

And I was happy to play it out there with all the other privileged fuckers who had everything that money could buy and yet wandered around hungrily trying to fill the empty void in their souls by spending recklessly, drinking too much, fucking everything with a heartbeat, and taking massive amounts of drugs.

2

Nico was slouched in his leather lounger watching TV when I walked into his room.

He looked up at me, and for the smallest fraction of a second there seemed to be a glimmer of recognition in his eyes. Then he gave a wolfish smile.

"You my new nurse?"

I played along. "Do you want me to be?"

He shrugged. "I've seen worse."

I laughed out loud. It was that or cry.

He laughed too. But then he said, "I'm just giving you a hard time. You are a beautiful woman. When I was much younger I would've pursued you with everything I had."

I blinked back my tears. "I bet you were something else."

"Oh, boy, was I," he said and frowned. "At least that's what I've been told."

Even having a picture of me hugging him on the dresser in his room wasn't enough to jog his memory of our life together. He might look at it for a few seconds but would then ask why and where we had taken it.

But as hard as it was for me, Rose couldn't handle it at all.

She'd taken every picture of us as a family and herself out of his room.

I don't even know if she still came to visit him. She wouldn't answer when I asked.

She was in a dark place, and I couldn't reach her.

I called her on my way over to tell her I was leaving Barcelona for a while.

She didn't answer her phone so I left a message. Typical.

"What's on the agenda today?" Nico said, standing. I tried not to notice him reach out to grip the arm of the chair to steady himself. He was frowning.

"I thought we would take a walk in the garden," I said. "Get a little fresh air and sunshine."

"That's what you all say."

"That's because it's good for you."

He shuffled over to me. Along with the decline in his mental health, he had grown frail over the past few years. It was just another knife in my heart.

I wanted to help him, but I knew his ego couldn't handle it.

Outside, we walked for a while and then sat on a bench near a row of flowers.

He looked over at me., wringing his hands. At first it had bothered me, but the nurses told me it was common with Alzheimer's patients, and I'd gotten used to it. It was, like everything about Nico now, including the colostomy bag, so unlike the man I'd loved for so long.

"Do I know you?" he asked.

I smiled. "Yes."

"I mean before this?"

"What do you think?"

He stared at me hard. "I get really confused sometimes."

"It's okay," I said in the most comforting voice I could. Sometimes when I was with him and he was confused, he would grow angry and violent. It scared me. But I also didn't blame him. I was pissed off too.

Then he shook his head. He turned and stared straight ahead and said, "Maybe in another life."

"I think you're right. In another life."

"Do you believe in that?" he asked.

"Of course. Don't you?"

I'd never seen anything in my life as beautiful as his smile just then. "Yes. Yes, I do."

I looked away so he wouldn't see the tears falling down my cheeks.

Suddenly, he stood.

"I'm tired, nurse," he said. "I'm sorry I don't remember your name. I forget most things."

"I never told you my name. It's Gia."

He nodded. "That's a nice name."

"Thank you."

"Can you show me back to my room? I think I should take a nap."

"I'd be happy to do that, Mr. Morales."

I used his real name to see if he reacted. He didn't.

After I tucked him into bed and pulled the curtains in his room, I gave him a kiss on the cheek as I said goodbye. He acted surprised by the kiss, his forehead wrinkling up and his eyes squinting.

Of course he did.

But then he immediately seemed to forget it.

"Sleep well, Mr. Morales."

He didn't answer.

As I walked outside to the waiting car, I wondered if it was the last time I was going to see the man I'd considered my husband for so many years.

3

When I stepped off the plane onto the tarmac, I paused and inhaled deeply. Even though Cannes was only a bit north of Barcelona, there was still something different about the air here. I don't know if it was knowing there were miles between me and my other life, but it felt like a weight had suddenly been lifted from my shoulders.

When we landed, it was as if the dark shadows fluttering and hovering around my peripheral vision had been banished.

"Ms. Santella?" A man with a goatee and longish bangs greeted me. Despite the Mediterranean heat shimmering on the tarmac, he wore tight black jeans and a black long sleeve shirt with the sleeves rolled up to his elbows, revealing dark, deeply tanned and muscled forearms. One arm had a tattoo that I recognized: it was a skull wearing a beret against a dagger. I also couldn't help but notice he wore expensive Italian leather shoes.

Dante had taught me to notice shit like that—the shoes, not the tattoo.

Dating James the cop had taught me to identify the tattoo. Green beret or Special Forces for sure.

"Ryder," he said, sticking out his hand and flashing a grin

that took me aback. That smile elevated him from average looking to dangerously attractive.

"Let me guess," I said, shaking my head with mock exasperation. "Dante sent you."

He laughed. "Only to get you safely to your villa."

"He acts like I'm still twelve sometimes."

I was pissed. And I wasn't sure why.

The man frowned. "Why, for hiring someone to drive you?"

"Oh, please," I said. "You're charming as fuck, but the 'driver' shit doesn't fool me for a second. I bet you have an ankle holster with a gun and another one in your glove box. I would bet my last dollar you are highly trained in some form of martial arts and could break someone's neck in thirty seconds."

He began to laugh, but I continued. "If you want to pretend you're simply a driver, I'd hide that tattoo," I said, squinting as I looked at him.

Now he laughed loudly. "Touché."

"Let's go," I said and walked past him.

He held the door to the back seat open for me, but I ignored him and went around to the passenger door. Once I settled into the passenger seat of the big black car, I stared out the window while he got in. I didn't want to talk to him. I'd planned on spending at least my first week here not talking to another soul, but curiosity got the best of me.

"How do you know Dante?" I said. I know I sounded crabby.

"Matt."

My mouth grew dry. I didn't answer. I couldn't speak, so I simply nodded.

Matt had been Dante's husband for all of a few hours when a gunman shot him and Bobby dead in Positano by the Tyrrhenian Sea.

"I was Secret Service when Matt was a senator," he continued. "Dante and I have stayed in touch."

"You have an accent," I said, keeping my eyes trained on the road in front of us. I wasn't sure how he could be Special Forces and Secret Service without being American.

"I was born in America, but my family moved to France when I was three," he said. "Before 9/11, it was considered desirable to have dual citizenship. Now? Not so much."

"Is that why you're here?" Despite my resolve not to talk the entire drive, I kept asking questions.

"I must say, I like it here a lot better than in DC," he said, avoiding my question. "I do private security here. Not as many rules."

He leaned over the steering wheel and pointed. "See over there? That's where your villa is. The area is called La Californie. Best part of town if you ask me. It's like your Beverly Hills. Very nice."

He was pointing to a hillside slightly above the village.

"I hope so for what they're charging."

"You must've reserved it, what? Two years ago? I heard reservations sometimes are three to five years in advance of the festival."

I shook my head.

The truth was I'd made the reservation last week. It had nothing to do with me and everything to do with my aunt, Eva Santella's, connections. As a former Italian mob boss and now leader of an all-woman army of assassins, she had connections in all the right places. But I didn't think Ryder needed to know any of that.

When I'd seen the pictures her contact had sent me, I replied, "Yes. Making deposit now."

I'd basically asked for a villa outside of town with breathtaking views of the Mediterranean, a massive swimming pool, and a full bar. Not a hell of a lot to ask, right?

Basically, what I wanted was a mini resort all to myself.

And as luck would have it, she found one.

"Believe it or not, I know your villa well. I have had many clients stay there. I know the owners personally. They live in Hong Kong most of the year. I didn't think it would be vacant right now with the festival in town."

I shrugged. "Beats me."

"Besides the festival, what else is there to do around here?" I asked as the car wound its way up the hill. I figured I might as well use him for information.

"Cannes is basically a bunch of celebrities showing off and fucking each other. Even during non-festival times."

I sat up. "Really? Tell me more?"

He laughed.

"I bet the really rich people bring their yachts here, right?" I said, looking out at bay.

"Really rich people?"

"What?" I said, confused.

"Because only slightly rich people rent the villa you're staying in. Please," he scoffed.

"I know. It's absurd. Trust me. I know."

Then he side-eyed me.

"What?" I said again.

"You don't act like the rest of them."

Then I remembered I didn't really like him and didn't want to talk, so I clamped my mouth closed.

Then he laughed even harder.

"But you're trouble. I can tell," he said.

I thought about his easy laugh, that smile, those strong hands on the steering wheel, and his extremely fit body and shook my head.

He was the one who was trouble.

When he laughed again, showing these brilliant white teeth, I frowned.

He must have seen it because he put both hands on the wheel. I could see out of the corner of my eye that he was staring straight ahead out the windshield.

"Definitely trouble," he said and snickered. I glared at him, and he had the audacity to laugh again. "I make a point to stay far away from women like you."

4

THE VILLA WAS TUCKED AWAY UP IN THE MOUNTAINS. THE LONG driveway made it feel even more secluded. Ryder pulled into the wide circle drive, put the car in park, and smiled at me.

"Here we are."

I looked around and felt a little panicked.

"It's really far away from..." I trailed off.

"Anywhere."

I bit my lip. I was a city girl. Always had been. Always would be. Maybe this wasn't a great idea.

He opened the driver's side door, and before I could react, he was over at my door, opening it for me.

I took a deep breath and climbed out, stretching.

The white stone façade of the villa that faced the driveway was impressive dotted with windows that belied its massive size, but as soon as we stepped inside, I saw what I'd been dreaming about.

I took out my cell phone and squinted at the directions for the alarm. It wasn't something I'd seen before. It gave instructions for how to program it with my own code.

"May I?" Ryder said. "I'm familiar with this system."

I handed him my phone.

Ryder opened up a small panel and pressed some buttons, glancing down at my phone.

"This alarm system is state-of-the-art," he said. "You're going to want to have it armed all the time, I think. We've had some daytime break-ins around here lately. One man was in his home office and came out to grab lunch, and a burglar was loading up a van in the driveway."

"That's brazen."

"Yes. So keep the alarm on while you are home. Especially since you will be here alone."

As soon as the door opened, I walked inside.

"Wait," he said. "We have to set your code..."

But I was already down the hall.

"I will show you how to program it before I leave," I heard him say behind me.

Inside, the ceilings stretched high above, and rooms were separated by curved stone archways. The décor was luxurious and yet cozy, big white plush couches with white faux fur throws and crystal candles and chandeliers. The black marble floors and mirrors on every wall were offset by velvet furniture and satin wallpaper in soft creams and pale pinks.

I followed Ryder through the house. He lugged my two suitcases for me as he headed up a steep set of wide, worn pink-and-white marble stairs. At the top of the stairs, he turned right, and at the far end of a hall, double doors opened up to the master suite. The entire wall to my left opened up to a wide balcony overlooking the backyard.

I rushed through the room and threw open the doors to the balcony. To my left were other balconies. Each room had one. The back of the house looked down on the bay below. It was magical.

Directly below me, surrounded by a gleaming white stone

patio lay a magnificent turquoise pool with a small waterfall feeding into it. A hot tub, nearly as big, sat off to one side. On the other side I spotted an outdoor kitchen.

The entire area was filled with lush, tropical trees, plants, and flowers. A large lawn led to a steep drop-off and more foliage. I could just spot the top of another villa far below.

Closer to the building was a stone patio scattered with lounge chairs, café tables, and umbrellas.

It looked like a small boutique hotel. Just what I had wanted.

And it was all mine.

I laughed out loud.

"I take it you approve?"

Ryder was by my side.

"Oh, yes."

I turned around and headed toward my suitcase, which he had set on the bed. I kicked off my shoes and began to shrug out of my T-shirt.

Ryder cleared his throat. I glanced over at him. He frowned and turned around.

"What's your problem?" I said.

"You're taking off your clothes." I tried to read his voice, but couldn't tell if he was amused or offended.

"Yeah, I'm going swimming."

"I can wait outside your room."

"Don't bother. I mean, um, I thought I was in the south of France? Maybe I landed somewhere else."

One thing I loved about Europe, particularly Southern France and Italy and Spain, was the lack of modesty. Nudity was no big deal. Entire parks in Germany were devoted to nudists.

As I rummaged in my suitcase for my white bikini, Ryder made a sound. I couldn't tell if it was a snicker or a huff of exasperation.

I glanced at where he stood facing the door, but he didn't

move. Shit. He wasn't even tempted to turn around and look? I'd lost it for sure. I was just some old married woman now.

Just in case, I threw my shirt across the room, and it landed on the floor beside him. Nothing. So I slipped out of my pants and tossed my lace panties on top of the shirt. He didn't even glance down. For some reason, I found this unbelievably irritating.

"I'M sure you've seen lots of women naked," I said, still trying to provoke him. "What's one more? I don't think you're a prude, so what's the deal?"

Then I noticed he was looking down at his phone. He wasn't even paying attention to me.

"Huh?" he said raising his head. "Will you need anything else before I leave?"

I ignored his question. I wasn't done talking about how prudish he was acting.

"That's one reason I came down here, so I don't have to put up with all the uptight bullshit."

"They sunbathe topless in Barcelona, too. I happen to have it on good authority." He said it matter-of-factly.

I made a face. I hated that he was calling me on my shit.

Then he walked out the door, saying over his shoulder, "I'll leave my number on the table downstairs."

And then he was gone.

"Don't bother," I shouted after him.

5

Swimming naked in the Olympic size pool was just what the doctor ordered.

After Ryder left, I decided to scrap the bikini and walked around the villa naked. I didn't even bother to grab a towel when I headed out to the pool.

The water was as warm as a bathtub and felt delicious.

I did several laps and was surprised when I popped up at one end to find a towel folded neatly on a chair and a large bottle of water with condensation dripping from it.

I glanced around quickly. Ryder was nowhere to be seen.

That was slightly creepy.

But I felt smug knowing he hadn't actually left when he'd said he was going.

Then I felt sort of guilty when I got out of the pool and trudged into the house only to find a plate of fresh fruit, cheeses, and meats laid out on the counter next to a simple white card with his name and number.

I picked up the card and examined it for a few seconds.

Just what was his story? All I knew is that he was one of the most annoying men I'd ever met.

Thinking this, I texted Dante.

"Your guard dog got me here safely. Is he a eunuch or what?"

I watched the bubbles on my phone screen that appeared as Dante wrote back. Then his text appeared. "What? He's all man, baby."

"Oh! He's on your team. Boy is my gaydar broken."

"Wrong. If he was, I would've brought him home years ago. What's your problem? By the way, using the word 'gaydar' is offensive and so 2017. And it's broken if you think he's gay."

"Whatever," I said. "He must be gay because he wasn't interested in seeing my boobs. And we both know I have great boobs."

"All I know is he's not gay. Maybe he has a girlfriend?"

"He still could've looked."

"Some men have integrity."

"Oh, yeah, I forgot."

I hadn't, actually. Nico was the epitome of integrity. But he was one of a kind.

Thinking of him made a heaviness fall over me. I glanced down at the plate that Ryder had prepared. It looked like a piece of art.

Definitely gay.

I stuck a piece of cheese and slice of nectarine in my mouth, and it tasted like heaven. I made a small plate of the food, reached for a bottle of red wine sitting near the platter, and headed back out to the pool.

I spent the rest of the afternoon listening to Eminem, Juice WRLD, and Cardi B, reading the latest Gregg Hurwitz thriller, and sipping wine.

The sun beating down on my body felt glorious. When I got too hot, I'd dive into the pool to cool off.

I checked my phone a few times and then decided to delete every single app on it except for my music apps. I was going off the grid. No more news. No more social media. I used to keep track of all that when Rose was younger, but now that she was out in the world on her own, I never used them anymore.

Thinking of Rose made a pit form in my stomach.

She was a warrior. A killer. But she was still a little girl to me in some ways. Still barely an adult. Still the girl I had met as a frightened eight-year-old. It was incredibly difficult to let go and let her make her own way in the world. Especially when that way involved hunting down sadistic cult leaders who sacrificed children. But I had no say in the matter.

Nobody could have stopped me at her age.

I knew I couldn't stand in her way. All I could do was love her and be there for her in any way I could at any time. All she had to do was say the word, and I would drop everything in my life to go to her and help her. She knew that. That was what I could offer. But it didn't feel like nearly enough.

Rose had my phone number. Dante had my phone number. Eva had my phone number. And the nurses at memory care had my phone number.

Other than that, there was no reason for anyone else to reach me.

I'd texted all of them during the day to let them know I was settled into the villa and planning on staying off the grid and reading and lying in the sun until the festival started the next week.

I was surprised at dusk when my phone rang.

It was Ryder.

"I'm out front."

"Okay..."

"I forgot to show you how to program the alarm. You have to set your own code."

"Oh, right," I said.

"May I come in?"

"Yeah."

I met him at the door with a robe on. It was the least I could do since he'd driven all the way back here to help me set the alarm code.

After he showed me how to personalize the code, he discreetly walked out to his car while I programmed my own personal pin. Then he came back and stood at the foot of the steps.

"I thought I'd take you to dinner. Reservations for C'est Bon usually need to be made weeks in advance, but I was able to get us in...the seafood paella is exquisite..."

For some reason the arrogance of his assumption that I would drop everything and go out to eat with him incensed me. I was positive Dante was behind this. Paying him to keep an eye on me. Or worse, paying someone to keep me company.

"Hey, no offense, but I came here for some solitude. Enjoy your dinner."

I closed the door without waiting for his response. At the last second, I set the alarm. Then I stomped around the first floor of the villa, keeping to the back of the house so I didn't have to see his car leaving.

After a few minutes, I peeked out a window to see if his car was gone. I couldn't see, so I went to the front door and cracked it. An earsplitting, God-awful screech erupted, complete with strobe lights and blaring sirens. I slammed the door shut and punched in my code. The noise stopped, and I stood with my back against the door, heart pounding.

Jesus H. Christ.

Then I set the alarm again, reminding myself not to open the door again no matter what and headed back to the kitchen. There, I opened up another bottle of wine. Upstairs, I unearthed a silver cigarette case from my suitcase. It contained several neatly rolled joints.

Fortified with weed and wine, I went out back.

The entire area was lit up turquoise blue with hidden lights in the pool and in the thick tropical plants and trees. This time, I played Mexican music—narcocorridos. The songs were basically drug ballads written by famous singers and dedicated to—and about—drug lords. It was music that Nico had always loved. One artist had even written a narcocorrido about Nico.

I found that one on my phone and played it, tears streaming down my face.

It always made me cry when I listened to it, and that's what I was going for. I was in a melancholy mood.

I drank wine, smoked weed, and sang along loudly to the narcocorridos as tears dripped down my face. Somewhere along the line I lay my head back on the chair and closed my eyes.

I woke later, shivering.

I'd fallen asleep in the thickly padded lounge chair. The music was still playing and the shimmering blue light from the pool was disorienting.

I trudged upstairs to my room and fell into the big plush bed, barely managing to pull the covers over me before I was asleep again.

THE NEXT MORNING, I woke up blinking at the bright sunlight pouring through the windows onto my bed. My head throbbed and my mouth was parched. When I rolled over, a wave of nausea overcame me. I froze, willing myself not to puke.

With my face buried in the pillow, I reached over to the nightstand, feeling for the bottle of water I'd seen there the night before. I had to sit up to drink it.

Once that feat was managed without barfing, I chugged

about half of the bottle before realizing the only thing that was going to work was some hair of the dog.

I pulled on a leopard print bikini—swimming naked had quickly lost its novelty—and headed downstairs, grabbing an extra-large pair of dark sunglasses before I went. In the kitchen, I dug through every cupboard until I found what I was looking for—the real booze.

I grabbed a bottle of tequila and headed for the pool.

The Mexican narcocorridos were still playing through the speakers, somehow still connected to my phone and playing on repeat. But I was no longer in the mood.

I dialed up some Marvin Gaye, uncapped the tequila and took a big swig and then another. I suddenly felt a little better. I lay back down on the lounge chair and slept for an hour, dreaming of the 1970s and wishing I'd been alive during that time.

I woke sweating and thirsty. I grabbed a bottle of tequila and another glass filled with ice water and headed for the pool. I sank into the refreshing turquoise water, tipped the bottle back, and let the cool liquid slosh into my mouth and over my face, finishing it in a few desperate gulps.

The rest of the day was a lot like the day before. I drank and nibbled on cheeses and salamis and grapes and let the Mediterranean sun beat down on me as I listened to music and read. I picked up Orwell's Down and Out in Paris and London and spent most of the day re-reading the book that I'd once loved and still found enjoyable.

The sun beat down on me and warmed my bones, but I wasn't sure it could reach my heart.

I felt nothing.

I'd expected to spend at least part of this time in solitude grieving. I thought I would mourn Nico. Or at least mourn the life I'd led with him and Rose.

But I felt cold inside. Or maybe not cold. Just numb.

At dusk, I decided to switch up my alcohol choices and went for a bottle of red wine. I decided that I needed some Edith Pilaf to match the vibe of the wine and the Orwell book.

It was a good choice. Lying on the lounge chair wrapped in a soft blanket, the wine warmed me as I sang softly along to the strains of Pilaf's voice.

Soon, I stumbled up to bed.

On the third day, spent the same as the first two, I was nearly sober when the sun set. I'd cut back a little on the booze and drank more water and ate some fruit and vegetables I'd found in a basket on the kitchen counter.

I sat in the lounge chair drinking sparkling water as the sky turned from tangerine to purple to velvet navy. It was beautiful and I'd spent three days doing exactly what I'd planned to do, so what was the antsy feeling I had?

I realized I was restless. Bored as fuck, actually.

And lonely.

I stood, letting the blanket fall onto the patio, and headed upstairs.

It was strange. I didn't know myself anymore. I'd spent the last four years caring for Nico. I'd lost sight of who I was when I wasn't a caretaker.

Even though it had made me feel guilty as hell at the time, I'd daydreamed of days like this, when the only thing I had to worry about was me. When I could spend long, lazy hours lying by the pool reading books, sipping wine, letting the sun soak into my bones, and not having a care in the world.

And now that I had it? Snorefest.

I would give anything to be back in Nico's tiny bedroom, snuggled up beside him on his bed with his arm wrapped around me while he still knew who I was. Even if it meant helping him get up to go to the bathroom. God, I missed that man so much.

And before that, our life in Mexico and San Diego and Barcelona... It all seemed like a dream now. Or rather, a book I'd read a long time ago.

But I refused to cry about it. Instead, I would hold those memories tight and cherish them.

Why should I mourn a life that most people only dream of having? I was damn lucky, and I would never let myself forget that. Never.

But that didn't mean I wasn't dying for company.

And sex.

Oh, God—to feel a man inside me. I was practically ravenous for a man's touch. I was like a horny teenager again. I hadn't had sex for years. It was insane.

I mean, Jesus, look at my reaction to Dante's bodyguard. I mean, if I really was honest with myself, I'd wanted to jump his bones. Looking at his tattooed forearms and tight ass in those jeans had stirred something up I hadn't felt in a long time—pure, unbridled lust.

And he wasn't even my type.

Hell, did I even have a type anymore?

I guess I'd find out tonight. Because I was going out. I had cabin fever in a villa in the South of France. I'd go out, find a hot guy and blot all my thoughts out with mind-blowing sex. I deserved it. I was done being celibate.

Smiling, I downed a glass of tequila and headed for the bathroom.

After a shower, I dressed in a sleeveless leather dress with a square neckline that fell to mid-thigh and hugged my curves but was loose enough for me to move because I was going to find a club and dance until I dropped. And then I was going to find a hot fuckboy and go back to his hotel and rock his world. Yup. That was the plan.

I grabbed my phone and cigarette case and headed downstairs.

I found what I was looking for on the counter next to a binder with information about the villa—keys to the vehicles that came with the villa. Cars. Bingo.

Inside the garage, I spotted it—a white Jeep—nestled among a few other obnoxious vehicles, including a Rolls Royce Dawn convertible.

I keyed the ignition of the Jeep and revved the engine. Perfection.

Out on the open road, I stepped on the accelerator and hugged every dangerous curve down to the strip, loving the wind whipping my still damp hair, cranking my dance music, and singing along.

Once I was down on flat ground, it didn't take me long to find the happening clubs. There was a strip that had sidewalks filled with people lined up to get into one club after the other. I cruised slowly, eyeing the crowds out front before I chose one.

It was a white brick building with a neon purple sign that said "Depravity." Yup. That said it all. I stopped the Jeep near the door. The crowd looked a little young, but the music was what I was going for. I wanted to dance.

The door opened and I heard pounding music and loud laughter.

I yanked the steering wheel and headed toward the valet stand.

6

THE VALET ESCORTED ME TO THE FRONT OF THE LINE, PAST THE long lines of hopefuls on the other side of the red velvet rope waiting to get into the club. The doorman was about to let a group in but as soon as he saw us approaching he held up a big meaty palm.

One of the girls in the front of the line who had to wait scowled and turned to see what the problem was.

Her eyes landed on me and narrowed.

"Who the fuck is that?" she hissed.

She had thick, shoulder-length blonde hair, huge sky-blue eyes in a round face, and cantaloupe-sized tits squeezed into a white scoop neck dress. She was American Pie gorgeous. Except for the nasty look on her face.

"Amanda!" her friend said.

I sized her up in an instant. While she was actually even prettier than her blonde friend—with silky reddish-brown hair, piercing green eyes with doll lashes, and a light sprinkling of freckles across a perfect nose—she was hunched over as if trying not to draw attention to herself.

I wondered why. The insecure posture deflected attention.

Was it because she thought she was heavy? She might have been a little chubby, but it was hard to tell since she seemed to be trying to hide her curves by wearing a silky, unstructured lime-green dress that hung mid-calf.

All of this was taken in within seconds as I breezed past.

The blonde sputtered her outrage even more.

The brunette spoke out again. "We're next anyway."

I could tell the comment cost her. She sort of winced after she said it, as if she wasn't used to standing up to her friend. It pissed me off. And then I got even angrier as the blonde glared at her.

Let it go, I told myself.

As I passed, I met the brunette's eyes and winked at her. The girl blushed.

Once I was inside the club, I ordered three shots of tequila at the bar. I downed them quickly and then headed to the dance floor, weaving in between the hot, sweaty bodies, swiveling my hips with my hands in the air above me and feeling the music seep into my body, touching my core.

I immediately infiltrated a group of young men with all the moves and big smiles. They were seriously good dancers. Soon, I lost myself in the music, closing my eyes and feeling bodies move with and against me and wishing the moment would never stop. It was shocking how good it felt to have another body touch me.

A year ago, Nico had gotten finicky and violent, so they'd moved him into the supervised section of the memory care home. That meant we slept in separate beds. Most of the time he didn't know me, so hugging and kissing was out of the question. Back then, most of the time, he'd been pissed off at the world. Over time, he grew physically weaker, but we'd never again share the intimacy of our bodies touching. I had no idea how much I missed being touched until I wasn't.

But on the crowded dance floor, we all rubbed against one another without judgement or offense.

A black man with an infectious smile and hard body soon became my only dance partner, matching my every move. Oh, he would do just fine. If he moved like that on the dance floor, I could just imagine him in bed. Holy fuck. We danced together until I thought I would faint. Finally, he leaned over and said in a soft, French-accented voice, "May I get you a water? I'm parched."

"Yes, please," I said and followed him off the dance floor. I was relieved. I was dehydrated and exhausted but wasn't going to leave the dance floor for anything. Until he said something.

"Jean Pierre," he said as we got to the bar.

"Gia," I said and grinned. "You are an impressive dancer."

I took him in now under the brighter lights of the bar. He was hot.

He saw my appraising glance and gave me a wry grin, and I knew he'd picked up on everything I'd been thinking.

"My boyfriend is a professional dancer so it's nice to hear that."

I was dismayed at the disappointment that coursed through me.

I laughed out loud. "He's a lucky guy," I said.

Jean Pierre gave a bashful smile and shrug.

We stood sipping sparkling water and watching his friends dominate the dance floor. They were all incredible dancers.

"You all gay?" I finally said.

"Yes."

I laughed again. Now I knew for sure—my gaydar was broken.

This time he joined me. "You looking for company?"

"It's complicated," I said. "But yeah, I guess I am."

He nodded and smiled. "Honey, I'm sure you won't have any problems finding someone. Easy as can be, doll."

I clinked my glass against his and said, "But it won't be easy to find someone like you, Jean Pierre."

"That is very true."

I ordered another tequila, which Jean Pierre insisted on paying for, and was just finishing it when he looked at his phone and then at the dance floor. His friends were over at a table.

"We are leaving now. We have another club calling our name apparently. Would you like our table? They are hard to come by this time of night."

I looked around. It would be nice to sit and watch people for a while before I hit the dance floor again. I needed a few more drinks.

"You bet," I said.

I'd just settled into my table when I saw the two girls from the line walk by. They were carrying drinks. They were with four other people. It looked like they were searching for an empty table. The blonde was scowling, which I was starting to think was her regular expression.

The table I was at was massive. It could easily fit all of them and me, too, with room to spare. I wanted to make up for any bad feelings that little blonde felt about me. I was so over bitchiness between women. My goal, especially after raising Rose, was to encourage female solidarity wherever and whenever I could.

The brunette spotted me and quickly looked away. I felt bad. Did she feel like a traitor if she smiled at me? I was so glad to be past all that weird female bitchiness.

The first step was to share my table.

Even though the blonde wouldn't look at me, one of the young men she was with did meet my eye as they passed. I lifted my finger and crooked it toward him. He looked behind him to make sure I meant him, and then he came over, tossing his long bangs nervously.

"Hey," I said and gave him a smile. He might be the fuck boy I was looking for after all.

"Hi," he said back.

"You guys looking for a place to sit?"

The music was loud so he leaned down, putting his ear close to my head. I brought my lips close to his ear and repeated it. He drew back and stared at me for a second as if he didn't understand what I was saying.

I tilted my head toward the rest of the empty booth.

He gave me a slow smile and then took off toward the direction where his friends had gone.

A few seconds later, they all trudged back, with the blonde bringing up the rear.

I smiled at her and her alone.

"Hi," I said to her.

She stared at me for a few seconds before she said it back.

I stood and let them in and then flagged down the waiter. I handed him my credit card. "Whatever they want tonight is on me."

I left my bag on the seat and went out on the dance floor, losing myself in the throb of the music and hot bodies around me until I had to come up for air again and go back to the table for water and more tequila.

They were all talking and laughing when I showed up but fell silent when I sat down.

I pushed the damp hair back from my face and smiled.

I took them all in. There were seven total.

From what I could tell, the guy with the floppy bangs was solo. Perfect.

His name was Conner.

He made the introductions by pointing each person out to me.

The pouty blonde was Amanda. The guy kissing her was Owen. He looked like a football player, stocky with short hair, broad shoulders, and big muscles.

The brunette was Hannah. Between Amanda and Hannah was Lucas, a tanned guy with sun-bleached hair. A tall, thin girl with sleek black hair pulled back tightly from her face was Sabine. She was hanging on an equally emaciated boy with short black hair sticking up everywhere and thick black glasses named Clint.

I noticed something odd. Even though Owen and Amanda were making out, Amanda was sitting closer to Lucas than Hannah was—much closer than the packed booth required. It was fishy. If I had to guess, I'd have said their thighs were pressed up against one another's. And maybe his one hand under the table was doing something they didn't want the others to know about. It was something about how stiffly they both were avoiding looking at one another.

There was a pause in the music. Hannah smiled at me. "Thanks for the drinks."

I lifted my own glass and held it up. "My pleasure."

"Yeah, thanks," Conner said. I met his eyes for an extra-long time and gave him a slow smile, raising my glass to his. He got the hint and smiled back.

Then Amanda drew away from Owen's mouth and turned to Lucas. He immediately ignored Hannah, who had been asking him a question, and turned to Amanda. I glanced at Hannah. She was looking down at her phone. I couldn't tell if she had noticed or was upset.

"Can I have a cigarette, bunny?" Amanda said to Lucas.

He reached for the pack on the table, well within her reach, and took out a cigarette, lit it, and then handed it to her. She inhaled prettily and looked over at me smugly.

It was so fucking obvious to everyone. I snuck another glance at Hannah. Now, she was looking morosely down into her drink. Amanda was fucking two of the guys at the table, and one of them was her friend's boyfriend. I felt so bad for Hannah but reminded myself it was none of my business. I wasn't here to get caught up in the drama among a group of friends.

"Want to dance?" I said, looking at Conner.

He didn't answer; he just stood and grabbed my hand, leading me to the dance floor. I was glad it was crowded because it gave me a chance to throw my arms above my head and press myself against his body. He ran his hands down my sides, and I closed my eyes, swaying to the music and allowing myself to feel my body and escape my thoughts for once.

When the song ended, though, I was ready to sit down. I'd been drinking too much.

I needed water.

Conner was sweet and held my hand as we walked back to the table.

I saw Amanda's eyes flicker to our intertwined hands as we returned and could tell she was not happy. She was obviously used to being the girl who held all the boy's attention within her orbit.

Oh, well.

We slid into the booth, this time with Conner next to me. Hannah and Lucas must've been on the dance floor because they came back to the booth right after us.

Hannah slid in next to Conner, but Lucas sat across from her, next to Amanda.

Hannah looked down at her phone again.

But Amanda was ignoring Lucas. She kept staring at me and Conner.

He had his head turned toward me and was playing with my hair. Pretty soon I'd tuned out everyone and everything else except him. He was telling me a story about how they'd all met in college several years ago—except for Sabine and Clint—who they'd met recently. I was caught up in his voice and touch...

But then Amanda made her move.

"Hey, bunny," she said to Conner. "Will you walk out to the car with me? I'm cold and want my sweater."

It took me a few moments to realize she was talking to Conner. But she reached over and touched his sleeve.

It took him a few moments to realize she was talking to him, as well. He blinked and slowly turned his head toward her.

"I will," Lucas said suddenly.

Hannah looked up at him in surprise.

"Um, I mean, I'm closer to the edge," Lucas said. "It's easier for us to get out of the booth, right?"

It was true. Amanda and Lucas were sitting at the edges of the booth.

Without answering, Amanda slid out.

I watched Hannah's face sink as they walked away.

They didn't return for a very long time.

When they did, Amanda's lipstick was gone. Her skirt was twisted, and her hair was mussed.

Even without Lucas looking like the cat that had eaten the canary, it didn't take a fucking detective to figure out what they'd been doing.

And still, Hannah gave him a bright smile when he slid into the booth next to her.

I hated it. I wanted to kill both of them: Amanda and Lucas.

Conner and I exchanged a look. He knew I knew.

Suddenly, Owen, who seemed to be the only one oblivious to what had just occurred, swore loudly. He was staring at his phone.

"Motherfucker. I can't believe this. This is total bullshit. They fucked up our reservation."

They all started talking at once. The music started up again so I only caught tidbits of the conversation, but it soon became apparent that they had just got to town that afternoon and were killing time until their rental house was ready. Owen had just found out that the reservation had been fucked up. There was no reservation. There was no rental. There was no place for them to stay.

The tension at the table was sky high.

"I think we need another round," I said to the waiter. "And a few pitchers of water."

After downing some water, I sat there nursing another tequila as they all bowed over their phones, searching for a place to stay locally.

After about forty-five minutes, Amanda threw her phone down on the table and said, "We're fucked."

Conner nodded. "There's not another available hotel room, VRBO, or flop house within two hours of here."

Hannah sank back into the booth.

To my surprise, Amanda reached over and hugged her. "I'm sorry honey. I know it was your dream to be here, but I don't think it's going to work out."

I lifted an eyebrow. Conner saw. "Hannah is a film student," he explained. "She worked two jobs all last year to afford this trip after winning two tickets to the festival. The rest of us are all just along for the ride. But for her, this is it—the dream-come-true thing."

Hannah gave an unconvincing smile and sat up straighter, shaking her head.

"It's okay." She shrugged her shoulders. "I'm still having a really good time with all of you."

I don't know if anyone else caught it, but her eyes darted to Lucas.

He didn't even really look at her.

My heart broke.

Don't do it, Gia. It's a bad idea. Keep your trap shut.

And still I said it, "Hey, I have this big villa up in the hills all to myself this week and, frankly, it's a little fucking lonely and creepy up there by myself. You are all welcome to crash there."

Hannah actually gasped. Amanda's eyes grew wide and then narrowed.

The guys all whooped. Owen threw his fist in the air and said, "Hells to the yes."

Amanda crossed her arms, pouting. I saw Owen lean down and whisper something to her. Her face reddened, and she said something angrily. Even with a free place to stay, she wanted nothing to do with me. Oh, well.

Conner squeezed my thigh, and I reached down and moved his hand even higher.

Hannah shook her head and blinked at me. "Are you sure?"

I nodded. "Yeah." I said and shrugged. Was I? Fuck if I knew. But it was a done deal.

I ordered another round and then paid the bill.

While we waited, I asked Hannah about film school.

She was so excited to be in Southern France. Not just in Cannes for the festival, but near the settings where some of her favorite movies had been filmed. Just up the coast was where *A Deadly Union* had been filmed, she said.

"Have you seen it?"

I shook my head.

"It's called *Noces Rouge* in French or *Crimson Wedding*," she said. "It is set in the most amazing limestone cliffs. The highest sea cliffs in Europe. I'm going to see them for sure."

She went on about the movie, giving me an in-depth synopsis. I loved her enthusiasm and listened avidly. When she was done, she took a deep breath and then looked at me as if she was embarrassed.

"Did I bore you?"

"Not at all," I said. "I loved hearing you talk about it. So cool."

She smiled.

"I'll watch it for sure."

A few minutes later, after downing my tequila, I stood.

"I'm beat. You guys are welcome to stay longer, though. I can give you the address and my phone number. That way you can show up whenever you want, and I'll let you in."

Conner immediately stood. "I'm coming with you."

Of course you are.

To my surprise, they all scrambled to their feet and said they were ready to go as well. They trailed after me out of the club.

Outside, at the valet, Conner stayed by my side and then hopped into my Jeep. I didn't mind. I saw Amanda scowl.

I waited on the side of the road for the rest of them to pile into their white Chevy Tahoe. Conner's mouth was hot on my throat, lifting my hair up, and making me sigh.

"You can't do that while I'm driving, or I'll drive right off a cliff," I said.

He laughed and sat back, but his fingers traced electric patterns along my thigh the entire drive back to the villa, sending shock waves through me. Somehow, despite this, I managed to stay on the road and keep sight of the oversized vehicle in my rearview mirror as the road climbed the hills leading to the villa.

7

ONCE WE PULLED INTO THE WIDE DRIVEWAY, I PARKED AND JUMPED out of the Jeep. Without waiting for Conner to catch up to me on the front porch, I tapped the code into the pad that unlocked the door and disarmed the alarm system.

I didn't think it was a good idea to give them the alarm code.

Conner shouldered a backpack and stood waiting with me as the others made their way up the stairs, carting suitcases and duffel bags.

"Holy shit," one of the guys said.

The dark-haired emo couple brought up the rear.

Once they were all in the foyer, I pointed toward the staircase.

"I'm in the room at the end of the hall on the upper right, but feel free to make yourself at home in any other bedroom. I think there are six or so, not sure. I'm going out to the pool for a while before bed. The refrigerator is stocked, and there's a full bar, too. Help yourself. Consider yourselves my guests and make yourselves at home."

I saw them exchange wide-eyed glances. It made me happy.

Especially when I'd heard that Hannah had saved all year for this trip.

They hesitated for a second and then made for the stairs. Conner paused. Then he dropped his backpack at the foot of the stairs and walked toward me.

I liked that he wasn't making any assumptions. I also liked how bold he was.

Shy or uncertain guys weren't going to do it for me. Not now. Not at this point in my life. I wanted take-charge men. I didn't have time or patience for anything else.

He took my face in his hands and kissed me hard, pushing me up against the wall until his entire body was pressed up against mine. After a while, I realized we were going to have to take it somewhere else or cool off. I wasn't ready to turn in for the night yet, so I placed both my palms on his chest and gently pushed him away.

"Easy, sailor. We've got all night."

He pulled back and stared down at my mouth, breathing heavily and shaking his head.

"Where have you been all my life?"

I laughed. "You were doing so well up until then. Save the lines for the girls who need to hear them."

We headed into the kitchen then, and I made us Mojitos and headed to the pool.

After a while, the others came outside with the drinks they'd made. I sat at the far end of the pool where there were two lounge chairs. The others gathered at the opposite end, sitting at the edge of the deep end with their feet in the water.

Amanda leaned over and said something to the others, and they all looked over at me and Conner, who was sitting on the lounge chair beside mine.

"What's your story?" Conner said. "You're clearly American. What brought you here? The festival?"

"Sort of," I said.

"Not the festival?"

I shrugged.

"I've been caring for my ill husband for the past few years, and this is a bit of a getaway for me. I thought I wanted to be alone, but..." I trailed off.

"Husband?"

I looked at him and nodded.

"That's tough," he said. I could tell he wanted to ask more. Like if I was still married. He glanced down at my left hand. There was no ring. There never had been.

Nico and I were not legally married. But he was my husband.

I didn't want to share more.

"I'm sorry. I know being a caretaker is really hard."

I looked at him with surprise.

Instead of answering, I nodded.

"How long have you been here? At the villa?" he said. I knew he was changing the subject.

"I made it three days alone," I said, not meeting his eyes. "I spent years dreaming of time alone. Not having to worry about anyone else. It was all bullshit. It wasn't what I actually wanted."

He pressed his lips together. "That happens to me a lot."

I squinted at him. "Oh, yeah?"

He grinned.

"What's the story with Amanda and Lucas and Owen?"

"Boy, you don't miss a beat, do you? Owen has been in love with Amanda since first grade."

"That sounds like a sweet love story. How long have they been together?"

"About a month. It wasn't so sweet at first," Conner said, running his fingers through his long bangs. "At least not for Owen—he came from a pretty fucked up household. His mom took off when he was a baby. His dad is a raging alcoholic. They never had money. He always had on hand-me-downs and sometimes smelled bad."

Conner shot me a glance. "I feel sort of bad even telling you this."

"I don't judge," I said.

He pressed his lips together. "I can tell. So Amanda would have nothing to do with him. But she was crazy about Lucas. Their families were friends. Country club members. Had dinners together and so on. But Lucas didn't want anything to do with her. Until high school. Then they dated briefly. But he broke up with her. I think it's because she cheated on him or something. I never got the full story. But it was ugly. Meanwhile, Lucas and Owen have always been best friends. Even when they were little. I think it was really hard for Owen to see Lucas with Amanda."

"I bet."

"That's when Owen came into his own. By high school, his dad had died and he went to live with an aunt for the summer. By senior year he came back all built from working out and driving a Porsche. He'd apparently inherited some life insurance policy. All the girls at the school wanted to date him. Even Amanda."

"Did they date?" I said looking over at the two of them. Amanda and Owen were now in the pool. He had her pressed up against the wall and their faces were close.

"Nope. She had some other boyfriend at the time. Then we all went off to colleges across the country. Well, a few months ago, we all graduated and were back in L.A. and ended up picking up right where we left off. And that's when Amanda and Owen started dating. We met Sabine and Clint at a party and found out they were planning to come to Cannes when we were so we made plans to travel together. And here we are."

"Hey," he said in a soft voice. "Enough about us. Sometimes I talk too much. You barely have said anything."

"It's fine," I said.

"Well, I'm glad that you are here and can relax and enjoy yourself for once. It sounds like you haven't done that for a while."

For some reason his kind words made me teary. I quickly looked away.

"I'm sorry," he said. "Did I upset you?"

I shook my head.

Then his mouth was on mine. He was a really good kisser. And very sexy. I let myself go for a few minutes and then grew self-conscious when it got quiet at the other end of the pool.

I pulled back and said, "I think I need to go cool off in the pool."

He laughed. "Me, too."

At one point, we were all in the pool together. Amanda went back inside first, saying she had to call her sister in LA about something. Then Lucas said he was going to go make some drinks for everyone in the kitchen.

It was none of my business. Hannah wasn't paying attention. In fact, she was deep in conversation. Her back was turned to the house, and she was smiling and talking animatedly to Owen and Conner. It was good to see.

I was talking to the emo couple. They were actually really nice. Art students who were leaving in a few days to study at the Sorbonne in Paris. They really had only met the others a few weeks before at a party in LA.

Amanda and Lucas had been gone about twenty minutes when my phone rang.

It was sitting on the small table by the lounge chair. I got out of the pool, dripping wet, loped over to the table, and picked it up.

It was the care home.

"Hello?" I answered, my heart pounding.

I saw Conner watching me as I headed toward the house.

It was about Nico.

Dripping water on the floor, I stood inside the French doors frozen, listening to the voice on the other end tell me that Nico might have pneumonia.

I closed my eyes.

My gut was churning. I was dizzy and grabbed for the marble kitchen counter.

This was bad. Really bad. But there was little I could do, she said.

"The doctor will see him in the morning, and I will call you to tell you what he says."

As I hung up the phone, I sat there feeling dread claw at my insides. Part of me wanted to pack my bag and fly back to Barcelona, but I knew that was overreacting. I would wait to see what the doctor had to say the next day and then decide if I should return home. I couldn't do anything back home except sit around, sick with worry. As all these thoughts raced through my head, I heard voices down the hall. It was Amanda and Lucas.

I figured they'd snuck off to some back room a long time ago, so I was surprised to hear them from where I stood in the hallway off the kitchen.

"Seriously, when are you going to man up?" It was Amanda.

He answered in a voice so low I couldn't make out what he said. I froze with my hand on the door handle to the bathroom.

"I'm not going to wait much longer," she said.

This time I heard him answer. "Be patient."

"If it doesn't happen tonight, it's over. I'll do it myself."

"She'll know it was you. You'll ruin everything."

"Don't you push me. Don't you tempt me. You have no idea

what I'm capable of."

"I'm not afraid of you," he said.

"You should be."

What the fuck?

Then I heard footsteps. Instead of ducking into the bathroom, I stood my ground. It was my villa. But they had obviously headed the opposite way.

Something criminal for sure. Hannah was sweet and trusting. Or at least that's how she'd seemed in the few hours I'd known her. I hated to see her get hurt. These two people, her boyfriend and best friend were plotting something. And it was no good.

BUT, as I reminded myself, it was none of my business.

Their friendship and dating drama seemed foreign to me.

I was so glad I was past those days.

No thank you.

I was over it.

Even though in my mind my marriage was over, and I was a free agent, that meant very little in the scheme of things.

From now on, no more entanglements. Booty calls? Check. Romance? Avoid. Relationships? No way.

Back outside, I saw that everyone was out of the pool. Amanda and Lucas were now outside and standing at opposite sides of the patio.

I sat down and reached for my drink.

Hannah was suddenly at my side.

"Don't mind Amanda's attitude. She's okay. Deep down, she's not all that bad." She perched on the edge of the lounge chair near me.

"I've got no issues with her personally." Even though I think she's a crazy selfish manipulative bitch.

"Oh," she said. "I just saw the look on your face earlier."

"She's definitely a piece of work," I said.

Hannah took a sip of her drink before answering. "She's my best friend. She's just prickly, but she's got a good heart. I know she's grateful you're letting us stay here. We all are. Thank you again. For all of this."

"Wouldn't want you to miss the festival," I said.

Hannah lit up when she talked about film making. She said that she'd dreamed of directing since she first saw *The Virgin Suicides*.

"One of Coppola's best," I said.

"Yeah. But I also love *Lost in Translation* and *Marie Antoinette*."

"*Marie Antoinette* is my least favorite Sofia Coppola flick."

Hannah drew back with wide eyes. "Impossible!"

I laughed.

"The scenery alone. But the costumes! The costumes! It won the Academy Award for that."

I yawned. "Fashion bores me. To tears."

"Well, that explains it."

"Not to mention I'm not a big fan of historical pieces."

"I'm not sure we can be friends."

I laughed again. I really liked Hannah. I wanted to tell her that if she just shed her insecurity, her true beauty would shine through. Because whenever she talked about her passion—film—she lit up and was stunningly gorgeous.

I thought about how Amanda's more obvious beauty was marred by her shitty attitude. And I wondered what the hell she and Lucas had been scheming about in the house.

"How long have you been seeing Lucas."

Hannah blushed. "Not long. Can you tell?"

I shook my head.

Just then, he came over and sat beside her on the edge of the lounge chair, slinging his arm around her shoulders.

"Hey, babe. Want another drink? I'm about to go refresh mine." He jiggled the glass of ice in his hand.

She frowned. "I thought that's what you were just doing in the kitchen."

He blanched for a second.

"Nah. I was using the toilet."

I stared at him. He quickly looked away.

"Sure," she said and handed him her drink with a falsely bright smile.

He left.

Hannah swiveled her head to find Amanda. When she saw the blonde sitting on the edge of the pool with her feet in the water splashing Owen, she turned back to me and gave a wan smile.

After a few seconds of silence, I said, "How did you win tickets to the festival?"

"I really only won tickets to see Sofia Coppola's film and the private party afterward."

I gave a low whistle. "That's pretty amazing," I said and meant it.

She blushed. "It's incredible."

"You weren't going to skip going just because you didn't have a place to stay were you?" I was trying to feel out the girl's mettle. Was she a pushover in other areas of her life beyond the boundaries between her boyfriend and best friend? Would she let her friends derail her dreams? I don't know why I wanted to know so badly.

She vehemently shook her head. "I would've figured out a way to come. Sabine and Clint have plans to head up to his aunt's house in Paris. Last night we discussed going there for a few days, and I was thinking I could take the train down that night or something. It would've been complicated, but I still would've gone. Staying here makes it easy."

"I'm so glad," I said.

"Plus, I didn't really want to be away from Lucas for that long."

"Why?" I asked in a matter-of-fact voice.

She visibly squirmed, cracking her knuckles and shrugging. "I don't know. It's sort of dumb. Even though we've known each other since we were kids, we just started dating. It's all sort of fresh and new."

"Wouldn't he have come with you?"

She looked away and shook her head. "He's not really into film. He said I should take Owen or Conner because he loves Coppola."

I thought about what I'd seen earlier. How convenient for him to say that. Was it so he could be with Amanda?

Lucas appeared with her drink and sat back down beside her, kissing her neck.

"I'm bored," he said in a low voice. "Want to go to our room?"

"Yes!" she said and jumped up. She turned to me with a guilty look.

"I'm going to bed in a few minutes, too," I said and yawned.

When I stood, all the others looked at me.

"Hey, I'm going to bed. I'll lock up and set the alarm system. There's been some break-ins recently. If you need to leave for any reason, just come knock on my bedroom door, and I'll let you out."

Yawning, I headed for the front door. Suddenly, Conner was behind me, wrapping his arms around me from behind and kissing my neck. I shrugged out of his embrace.

"You are amazingly hot," I said. "But not tonight."

"Was it that call you got?"

It was none of his business, but after we'd been so hot and heavy earlier, I thought he deserved my honesty. I gave a slight nod.

He gave a small smile. And then did the sweetest thing—he kissed my forehead.

"Sleep well."

And then he was gone into the dark of the rest of the house.

I set the alarm system and headed up the stairs to my bedroom.

In my room, I slid the deadbolt across the door and stripped off my clothes without turning on any lights. The room had a faint blue glow from the lights in and around the pool below filtering in through my windows. With the French doors to my balcony thrown open, I could hear the others talking and laughing down below, and it was oddly comforting. A light breeze blew the long, sheer curtains into the room, and I felt a sense of peace I hadn't felt in a long time.

I fell asleep almost immediately.

I woke in the dark, sitting up straight. I'd heard a sound.

Something disturbing that sent my heart racing and blood pounding.

I wasn't sure what I'd heard, but it put my body on high alert.

Instinctively, I reached for the gun in my nightstand drawer.

My hand groped at an empty wooden rectangle.

It wasn't there. Neither was the silencer.

I switched on the bedside light to make sure, but the drawer was empty.

Then I heard a blood-curdling scream coming from the pool area.

I raced to my balcony.

Despite the sun creeping over the horizon to the east, the backyard was still in dark shadows, and the turquoise lights still lit up the pool, showcasing a horror vignette: a body floating in the pool surrounded by a crimson cloud of blood.

It was Lucas.

8

AMANDA, DRESSED IN A WHITE NIGHTGOWN, STOOD BY THE SIDE OF the pool, her body shuddering as she wailed.

Behind me, I heard doors slamming open and people shouting and footsteps.

I stood still for a second and then saw something that I wasn't sure how to interpret.

Amanda looked around, her head swiveling, and then she waited a few seconds very calmly. And then she screamed again.

What the fuck was that about?

Conner came racing outside, swore, and dove into the pool. He swam to Lucas's body, which was floating face down and pulled it to the stairs. He lifted Lucas out and put him on his back. He started CPR, but Lucas's face was blue. Even from the second story I could see that.

And still, Conner pumped on his chest. Owen was there suddenly, kneeling beside and shaking Lucas.

I reached for my phone and ran out of my room even though I was only wearing underwear and a thin camisole.

Outside, Conner had given up on the life-saving measures. He sat with his head in his hands on the edge of the lounge chair weeping. Amanda was sitting near Lucas's head, legs splayed, tears dripping down her face. Owen had his arm around her. He wasn't crying anymore, but his eyes were swollen and red.

"What happened? How did this happen?" she asked.

I grabbed a blanket out of a basket near the fire pit and gently covered up Lucas's body, trying not to meet his blue, sightless gaze.

I took Amanda by the arm. "Come on, let's go inside." She didn't fight me.

Owen stood, too, and put his arm around her. They headed for the back door. I went over to Conner. "You okay?"

He shook his head. "I don't understand."

"Me, either," I said. "Will you wait here while I call the authorities?"

He nodded, staring straight ahead.

I looked down at the cell phone in my hand and hesitated. I didn't even know who to call. What was 911 in France?

Then I realized I needed to call Dante's friend, Ryder.

He answered immediately.

"I've got a problem."

INSIDE THE HOUSE, I went back upstairs to put on pants before the cops came and found Sabine standing in front of Hannah's door.

"Something's wrong with her," Sabine said looking at me, white-faced.

I looked into the room. Hannah was sitting up in bed, bleary-eyed and blinking.

"What's going on? I don't feel so good."

She reached over the side of the bed and grabbed a small

ceramic trash can. She held it for a second and then leaned over and vomited into it

I sat on the edge of the bed and held her, pulling back her hair as she got sick.

Then she was done and thrust the trash can at me.

I set it on the floor and she looked at me.

"I can barely keep my eyes open," she said and slumped over. "Where's Lucas?" she said and then closed her eyes.

Sabine gave me a look.

"Did you see outside?" I asked her in a guarded voice. Sabine nodded and her face crumpled.

After I stood, I saw the glass near Hannah's nightstand. I lifted it to my nose and smelled it. It smelled like booze. Drugs? I wasn't positive, but Hannah's symptoms made it appear as if she'd been drugged.

Sabine helped Hannah downstairs while I went to throw on some sweatpants.

When I came downstairs everyone was in the great room except Conner and Lucas, of course.

The wide-open space contained three white leather couches flanked by marble tables. The group of friends sat slumped on the couches, their feet either curled up beneath them or propped up on the marble coffee table, which held the black onyx bust of a woman. Some sipped coffee. Some drank alcohol from crystal tumblers. Owen was drinking out of a black bottle —some type of booze.

I glanced at the bottle of alcohol on the coffee table. It was a bad idea to be drinking before the cops came, but what could I say? They'd just found their friend dead.

Immediately, my gaze found Hannah. She was seated between Sabine and Clint. Hannah was leaned back on the couch with her eyes closed, but she lifted her head when I walked in. Her head swiveled as she seemed to take everyone in around her. Then she looked at me and blinked.

"Where's Lucas. Where's Conner?"

They hadn't told her yet. Fuck me.

Sabine kneeled in front of her.

"Lucas is dead, Hannah. I'm so sorry."

"How? What?" She tried to stand but immediately fell back onto the couch when her legs buckled out from under her.

"We're not sure," I said.

"Where is he?"

"He was in the pool."

"Oh my God! Oh my God!" she said and tried to stand again. "I need to go to him. I need to see him."

"I don't think that's a good idea," I said. "Conner is with him."

I waited for her to ask how he died, prepared to give a vague answer, but the question never came.

Hannah looked at Amanda, eyes narrowed. "Who found him?"

She knew. I'd wondered how she could not know. Of course, she knew. She knew they had something–whatever it was—secret between them. Her tone was angry and vicious and accusatory.

"Amanda did," Sabine said and cast a worried look at Amanda.

"Of course she did." Hannah bit out the words as if they were venom.

We all looked over at Amanda.

She stared straight ahead, tears streaming down her face.

Suddenly, she stood and ran out of the room.

Owen looked around wildly at all of us and then got up.

But I beat him to it and held my palm out toward him.

"I'll check on her."

He sat down quickly. I could tell he was relieved. I wanted to talk to her alone, before the police came.

I found her out by the pool. She was curled on the pavement by Lucas's body, which was still covered with the blanket. Conner sat in a lounge chair nearby, smoking a cigarette, his hand shaking wildly.

I put my hand on Conner's shoulder.

"Why don't you go inside now?"

"I don't want to leave him alone."

"I'll stay with him," I said. I squeezed his shoulder. I didn't know what else to do. We both watched Amanda.

"I'm so sorry," she was saying.

I froze, but she looked up at me, her head jerking so her eyes met mine.

"Amanda?" I asked, as if I hadn't just heard her apologizing to a dead body.

"I know," she said. "I know...he's not really here anymore."

"What made you come out here this morning?" I asked.

She looked back down at him, her hair hanging in a curtain and hiding her face.

"It seems pretty early for you to be up after we were all up so late," I said, pressing the issue.

"I'm a morning person."

"So...you, what, just came out for a swim in your nightgown?"

I eyed the filmy white gown with the low-plunging neckline.

"Maybe," she said snottily. "What are you getting at?"

"Just trying to figure it out. These are the same things the police are going to ask you in a few minutes."

She looked up wide-eyed.

"Yeah," I said.

Then she was gone.

I watched her back as she disappeared into the house. She

didn't like the idea of the police questioning her, did she? Why was that?

When I turned back around, Conner was still sitting there.

"Sadly, he's not going anywhere, Conner. Then there's no need for anyone to be out here anymore. We'll make sure nobody comes out until the police arrive."

He nodded and stood.

Inside, Amanda was sitting demurely on the couch, again staring off into space. In her defense, everyone else was as well. I suspected that along with the shock, they were probably all sleep deprived and slightly hung over.

"Was it an accident?" Hannah's voice broke the silence.

I shrugged. I mean it was plausible that he'd hit his head and fallen in. But I didn't think so. Call it gut instinct.

"Not, it wasn't a fucking accident," Amanda said loudly and glared at Hannah. "You know that."

Hannah gasped. "I don't know anything."

"Bullshit."

"What are you trying to say?" Hannah said, her mouth dropping open.

"Why don't you tell the others about your little argument last night?"

"What the fuck?" Owen said.

Everyone started talking at once.

Then everyone froze and fell into an uncomfortable silence when the doorbell rang. I jumped up to punch in the alarm code and open the door.

It was Ryder.

He strode confidently through the room and toward the back of the house. Thank God.

As annoying as he was, it was nice to not have to be the only fucking adult in the room.

I stood quickly to follow him but first turned to the group. "Stay here. If the police knock, let them in and yell for me."

Then I led Ryder toward the back door.

"Who are your friends?" he said as we entered the kitchen. "And who is?" He waved his hand toward the blanket. The dead body.

"Long story short—ran into these kids at a club, was feeling lonely... Their reservation had been fouled up. I invited them back here. We stayed up late drinking. I woke to one of them dead in my pool."

He stared at me.

It sounded about as fucking strange as it was. I knew that.

I wasn't going to make an excuse.

I'd saved the best for last:

"And my gun and silencer is missing out of my nightstand drawer."

I could see him working the inside of his mouth with his teeth, thinking.

"Yeah," I said.

"Was he shot?"

"No idea," I said. "His friend did CPR, but after that I tried to keep them away from the body. I didn't really examine it."

He nodded. "Probably a good idea."

9

On our way back in, Ryder stopped at the kitchen and poured three fingers of tequila.

"Breakfast?" I said smiling.

He didn't smile back. He slid the glass across the black granite counter toward me.

I made a face. He raised an eyebrow.

I picked up the glass and downed it.

"Ready?" he asked.

Back in the living room, I stood by as Ryder took charge.

"The police inspectors are going to want to speak to all of you individually," he said.

"Why?" Hannah said, her voice shrill. "It was an accident. He must have had too much to drink, hit his head, and fell in the pool and drowned." She looked around wildly at the others and then her gaze settled on Amanda. "You were the reason he was drinking so much. This is all your fault."

Amanda jumped off the couch and became a blur of flying blonde hair and long pink talon nails scraping at Hannah's face. Both women were screaming. Before I could get there, Hannah had flipped Amanda onto her back and had her hands around Amanda's neck. The blonde's eyes were bulging.

"You wanted him so badly," Hannah said. "Now you can have him, you bitch. You could have had him for the past ten years. You never wanted him until I did. That's because you never wanted me to have anything. Ever since we were little, you've always had what I wanted—the clothes I wanted, the toys I wanted, the vacations I wanted, the boys I wanted. Why couldn't you let me have this one thing? All I wanted was him. I've given you everything our entire friendship. All I wanted was him. Why didn't you let me have him?"

Tears dripped down her face.

I watched. I knew I should do something, but I was too interested in what Hannah was saying.

Ryder was now in the room and pulled Hannah off of Amanda, who sat up holding her neck and gasping for breath. Everybody else appeared to be in shock, stunned into immobility.

Then the doorbell rang again.

Sabine went to Amanda's side to check on her. I glanced at Ryder. He jutted his chin toward the door, and I nodded.

While Ryder headed toward the front door, I took Hannah by the arm and led her into the dining room.

"You okay?" I said.

"No," she said. "I'm not fucking okay."

"I know," I said. "But you have to get your shit together now. The police are here, and they are going to want to talk to you. You have to calm down. You have to think. I need you to remember everything you can about last night. I think maybe you were drugged. I would tell them this and maybe ask for a blood test. And make sure they check that glass by your bed."

She bit her lip and nodded. A tear slipped down her cheek.

"Who do you think did this?" Hannah asked.

I shook my head and pressed my lips together.

"Did he have any enemies? Anyone you can think of? Did he piss anyone off since you guys got to Cannes? Maybe someone who followed us here?" I wasn't sure if someone could have gotten in from the backyard. It was basically on the side of a hill-side cliff, but maybe if someone wanted to badly enough?

"I don't know. I don't think so," she said.

"I'll have to talk to Ryder, but I think it would be pretty hard for anyone to get into the house at night. That alarm is shrill. Can you think of anything at all from last night that struck you as odd?"

She frowned. "Maybe."

"What was it?"

"I saw Amanda and Owen arguing right before bed. He went up to bed. She went out to the pool by herself."

"Then what?" I asked.

"Lucas and I went up to our room..." she trailed off.

"They argued. But it sounds like you did, too. Amanda said you and Lucas argued last night." There it was.

Hannah looked down. "We did. It's the same argument we always have. I get jealous. He reassures me that he wants me, not Amanda. He says he could've been with Amanda for years but never was. It's my own insecurity. Now, every time they talk or hang out, which they've done for years, I get jealous."

"Do you remember anything after you and Lucas went up to your room?"

Her eyes grew wide. "Yes," she said and nodded. "It was late. I remember Lucas getting out of bed and saying he needed to go get something to eat from the kitchen."

She sat up straighter. "I told him I was thirsty, and he brought us something to drink." She looked over at me. "That's the glass on my nightstand. Do you think we were poisoned?"

I frowned.

"Do you remember anything after that?"

"No," she said. "Not until Sabine woke me up and told me."

Her lip curled, and she began to sob.

Ryder reappeared in the doorway. I could hear voices from out at the pool. They must be out examining the body.

"The inspectors are asking everyone to stay in the living room, and they will call each person one-by-one to question," he said, giving me a glance. "I told them they could use the study."

"That makes sense," I said. "Thank you."

They started with me in the little study off the kitchen. It was filled with a large glass desk, potted plants, and prints of Paris maps. A large window overlooked the backyard, but showed the fire pit area, not the pool.

The detective behind the desk rose to greet me. He was heavyset with a buzzcut and a long, droopy moustache. But he had a friendly smile, which was disarming. Probably on purpose.

"I am Commissaire Boucher."

"Giada Santella," I said, using my full name for some reason. We shook hands and sat down. He settled into the massive, wheeled white leather office chair, and I sat in one of the orange leather chairs facing the desk.

"Where should we start?" he said.

I was taken aback but didn't let it show.

"I came here to relax. A vacation of sorts. I met the kids at one of the clubs in town last night. Their reservations fell through. I felt bad and offered to let them stay here. This big villa was getting a little lonely anyway."

"Kids? How old are you?"

"I guess I'm only a few years older than they are," I said. "Maybe I just feel older."

No maybe about it. I'd lived lifetimes compared to them. Then again, that applied to people older than me as well.

Then I told him how I'd spent the evening with them and then woke to the dead body. I also told him how I set the alarm every night before bed with my own special code.

"Did you see anything suspicious last night?"

"There was an interesting conversation between the victim and one of the young women."

Boucher tilted his head and lifted an eyebrow.

"I'm not sure it means anything. It was something about him having the balls to 'do something or she'd do it herself.' Or something."

I knew I was leaving a lot out. Like how he'd said he wasn't afraid of her.

I sighed heavily.

"There was something else," I said. "She told him he didn't know what she was capable of and his response was that he wasn't afraid of her."

Fuck. Was I throwing Amanda under the bus for something that could have nothing to do with the murder?

"Do you have any idea what they were talking about?"

"None whatsoever." I stood. I was done. I'd done my fucking civil duty. I wasn't sure why I felt so dirty about it. I felt played. I didn't know why.

I had my hand on the doorknob.

"We're almost done here," he said. "If you don't mind. A few more questions."

I turned back toward him.

"You said you set the alarm before turning in to bed," he said looking at his notes on the desk in front of him. "Is there any chance someone could have come into the house while you were sleeping?"

"I don't think so. When I accidentally set it off the first day, you could probably hear it down at the harbor. It's crazy obnoxious."

"And nobody else has your code?"

"Not a soul."

"My understanding from Ryder is that the alarm system doesn't cover the back of the house."

"That's dumb," I said.

He didn't answer only continued to take notes. I waited until he looked up at me again before I spoke.

"You seem to already be treating this as an investigation."

"It is," he said, a small smile on his face. "It's a death investigation."

He was avoiding what I was getting at.

"Have you determined the cause of death yet?"

"The coroner is working on it as we speak."

"Do you think he was murdered?" I finally said, putting it out there.

The detective met my eyes. "Do you?"

I waited a few seconds without looking away and shook my head.

"Why?" he asked.

"I know killers," I said meeting his eyes. "I just can't see any of them as murderers. Maybe I'm naïve..." I trailed off and shrugged.

His gaze was piercing. I made sure I wasn't the first one to look away.

"We haven't ruled out that it was someone who came into the house. They might have come up from the canyon into the backyard."

I paused. He was obviously familiar with Ryder and had talked to him before he arrived. That was unnerving. I realized I needed to tell him about my gun. I did so quickly.

"Was your door unlocked when you weren't in there?"

I nodded. "It only locks from the inside."

"Aha," he said and scribbled more notes. Then he looked up.

"I think that is all for right now," he said. "Thank you for your time. Please stay in town until we complete our investigation."

"What?" I turned back around.

"It would be best if we could keep track of everyone for the next twenty-four hours at the very least. We can't make you stay in Cannes, but I am asking you to do so. I'm going to ask the others to surrender their passports. You are an EU citizen, so I can only ask you to please stay until we know more. Can I count on your cooperation?"

"I'm going to have to get back to you on that."

He frowned and I walked out before he could respond.

It was a long day. Hannah spent the day curled up in the fetal position on a small loveseat, her red eyes staring off into space. Amanda sat on the couch, breaking out into sobs every once in a while. Owen had his arm around her and his chin on top of her head. Sabine sat on the floor by the loveseat, occasionally reaching up to pat Hannah. Clint sat in a chair nearby on his phone.

One by one they were brought into the study.

Amanda was right. It had to be an accident. Lucas had to have had too much to drink, fallen and hit his head, and ended up in the pool. The way they cried and took care of each other, it seemed there was no way one of them could have done this. But who knew?

However, I did keep thinking about the conversation I'd overheard between Lucas and Amanda.

But seriously, she was a spoiled brat, but hardly a killer. Probably the worst she'd done was sleep with her best friend's boyfriend, which was highly likely from everything I'd seen.

I paced most of the day feeling helpless.

Ryder stayed in the kitchen, busy on his phone or a laptop he'd set up at the bar counter. He made food for everyone—

sandwiches and fruit that remained largely untouched—and kept handing out bottled water. Around two in the afternoon, he brought out a tray of drinks and everyone reached for one. Then he brought out two bottles—one of tequila and one of whiskey. We all had several shots. Once again, I thought about how different everything was in Europe. In the states, a room full of grieving friends or even possible suspects wouldn't be served drinks.

As soon as she downed hers, Hannah immediately rushed to the bathroom. A police officer stationed at the door to the living room initially tried to stop her, but Ryder scolded him in French. The officer stepped aside, but followed her down the hall. Another officer immediately took his place. I didn't like that.

Were we prisoners here?

I stood and headed for the study. A burly guy in a gray police-issued sweater stood there looking bored.

"I need to speak to the commissaire."

When I was led into the study, I was pissed. "Listen, your men are following us to the bathroom? What's up with that?"

I stood before him with my arms crossed.

I had no idea what the rules were here in France, but this was utter bullshit.

I'd been trying to be helpful, but this was too much. Not to mention, every time I walked into the kitchen, I still could see Lucas's body by the side of the pool. All by itself.

"And what the fuck? Do you just let bodies sit there and rot in the sun?"

The detective started to roll his eyes but then said, "It's complicated. He is not French, no?"

"No," I said in an irritated voice.

"We have the coroner submitting a report and notifying American embassy about procedure and other details. It's very complicated. International."

I chewed on that for a few seconds. "Fine. But I refuse to be treated as a prisoner or a suspect in my own home."

"Your own home?" He raised a thick black eyebrow.

"Whatever. The place I'm renting."

I walked out.

Instead of going into the living room, where everyone was staring morosely at their phones, I went into the kitchen. Ryder was there, perched on a bar stool and typing on his laptop keyboard. I wondered what the hell he was doing all day long on his computer. I thought he was a bodyguard or something. I got a quick glance at his screen. Aha. He was writing something in a Word doc.

For some reason, I found him less annoying, knowing that.

Without a word, I reached for the tequila bottle, poured a shot, downed it, and poured another. I reached over to a cigarette pack on the counter and extracted one. Before it had barely touched my lips, Ryder put a lighter to it.

"You okay?" he asked.

"How long is this going to take?"

He turned away from the computer to face me. "It seems like they've done everything they can here. I'm not sure."

I slumped on a bar stool. "I just want to be alone, but now he's saying that they have to stay here for at least twenty-four hours. Not that I'd have the heart to kick them out anyway. What the hell? They are so young. And their friend was just killed. Maybe murdered."

"Have they determined that?"

"The detective won't say shit, but yeah, that's what I think is going on. But I seriously can't imagine one of these kids killing their friend. Is there any way someone could've got in? Like up the canyon behind the house."

His eyebrows knit together. "Yes. It is possible. Very ambitious. But possible."

"Here," Ryder said, pushing a plate of olives and cheese toward me. "Eat something."

I idly picked at the plate and ate one green olive and a slice of cheese and pushed the plate back at him.

"Ha!"

"I'm not hungry."

He eyed me. "I didn't think you were one of those ridiculous girls who don't like to eat."

I gave him a disparaging look. "Hell, no."

"Then eat."

"There's a dead body within my view. I think that's a pretty damn good excuse not to eat right now."

He shrugged. "Eh? Probably."

Just then there was a ruckus in the other room: voices and footsteps and doors opening and closing. I stood up.

Lucas's body was no longer out by the pool.

They'd finally taken it away.

Ryder grinned at me. "Now you have no excuse not to eat."

I made a face.

The detective poked his head into the kitchen.

"We are done here. I just told the others that they'll need to remain here for another day or so until our investigation is complete. I have confiscated all of their passports."

I stared at him, daring him to ask me again for mine. He didn't.

"Was it an accident?" I said.

"No," he said. "It appears to be a homicide."

10

Everyone had retreated upstairs when the police had packed up and left. But as night fell, people slowly emerged from their bedrooms.

Ryder had gone home after I refused his offer to stay and provide protection.

"It is my job," he said. "I am a highly paid private security officer. I will stay for free."

"Gee, thanks," I said sarcastically but followed it with a grin. "I think we'll be okay."

He chewed on his lip for a second before replying.

He reached into a briefcase and took out a small gun.

"I'd feel better if you kept this on you and slept with it near your bed," he said and slid it across the counter toward me. "I assume you know how to use it."

I glanced down at it for a second and nodded.

The detective had refused to tell us the cause of death. Maybe Lucas had been shot. After all, my gun was missing along with my silencer. That might have been the sound that woke me. It had only been twelve hours. It felt like a lifetime.

I had napped in my room most of the early evening. I hadn't

realized how exhausted I was. I was a loner, and simply having all these people in my space would've required some down time, but dealing with a dead body and trying to keep everyone consoled since I was the closest thing to a parental figure in the house? It had drained me.

It had been nice to have Ryder there. I appreciated him showing up and offering to stay. To my surprise, I didn't find him annoying at all anymore. Who knew why?

Standing at the French doors to my balcony, I looked down on the patio.

Everyone sat around the pool nursing drinks. They were talking in low voices and there was music piping out of the speakers. It was somber. I wondered what they were talking about.

I thought about shooting Dante a text to ask how much he was paying the guy to be my bodyguard or spy on me or whatever he was doing. But I didn't want to have to explain to my best friend that there had been a murder. If Ryder hadn't said something to him, I sure as hell wasn't going to be the one to bring it up. And I was certain Ryder hadn't because if he had told Dante, he'd have already called.

Then I froze. Unless. Unless he had told Dante and my friend was already on his way.

Part of me wanted to fall into Dante's arms for emotional support, and part of me wanted to do this on my own.

I'd grown a bit too dependent after years spent with Nico as my rock.

It was only in the past four years that I'd started to find my way without him again.

It's crazy how easy it was to lean on someone else once I gave him my whole heart and soul. But now, it was back to square one.

I could only rely on myself.

Nico was the only man I've ever had in my life who seemed stronger than I was. Besides my dad, of course. But my mother was always the stronger of the two when I think back.

But as far as lovers, there was nobody I felt I could turn everything over to like I did Nico.

Bobby was sweet and innocent. He was someone I felt like I had to protect. I never felt like I could turn to him for help with my deepest fears and concerns. But I loved that man more than anything. James, my badass cop boyfriend, was someone I could rely on. But he never really knew me. He didn't want to accept that I'd killed people. I always had to keep a guard up around him. I always felt that if he knew what I was really like, he'd despise me. And even so, my history, my track record as a killer and vigilante, had ultimately driven us apart.

But when I met Nico, he loved me for who I truly was. He knew I'd killed. I knew he had, as well. We met as equals and accepted each other's flaws and shortcomings.

And at the same time, I felt like he could protect me. He was stronger than I was. At first it made me uneasy. I was used to being the strong one, independent and on my own. But over the years, I got used to it.

He always treated me as an equal, but I didn't have to always be on guard. I didn't have to worry about everything quite so much. I knew that Nico was there to keep our family safe.

For the most part, we were safe, hiding in Barcelona, but there was that one time...

We'd managed to keep it from Rose.

She was still a pre-teen at the time.

We'd sent her to visit Eva so she didn't suspect anything.

Django, the best dog in the world, was still alive.

He was the one who saved our lives.

Nico and I were out on the balcony having a drink. Rose was

at a sleepover at her friend's house. It was a rare night when we had the place to ourselves.

The living room of the Gothic Quarter apartment was lit with candles, and some narcocorrido music played softly on the stereo. Nico was singing along softly, and we were both laughing, feeling giggly and in love.

Despite the late hour, the streets of the quarter were still filled with people talking and laughing. Barcelona was such a vibrant city. At the time, I remember thinking that nobody could feel lonely living there. That was before I lost Nico.

We had our feet up on the balcony railing and were talking about some of our adventures in Mexico. How so many people had tried to kill us, and we'd thought we'd have to live in hiding forever, and yet, we'd been in Barcelona for years and lived a peaceful life.

Famous last words, right?

I went back into the apartment to grab some bottled waters for us when I heard and saw something that made my blood run cold.

Django, who had gone to bed early, bereft that Rose wasn't there, was now standing in the doorway of her room. A low, deadly growl thrummed from his throat, and his fur was standing on end. He was facing our bedroom.

A dark form materialized just as I reached off to the side and plucked a poker out of the stand near the fireplace.

Everything happened at once and seemed to be in slow motion: The figure wore a creepy, skin tight outfit from head to toe. With the exception of the two eye holes, every inch of the person's skin was covered in black. Whoever it was lunged for me. I screamed a bloody war cry as I braced myself for the attack. At the same time, Django erupted into a bone-shattering bark as he flew through the air, fangs bared.

The three of us made contact at the same time. Django clung

to the figure's rubber-clad leg. I managed to spear the left side, but only barely as the person had dodged my thrust and come down on my shoulder with some type of heavy rod that sent me to my knees, reeling in pain. The man howled and yanked the poker out, sending it flying. It landed a few feet away, clattering to the floor.

I scrambled to my feet and jabbed my right knee into his groin. The resulting grunt confirmed my theory that I was dealing with a man.

I'd hurt him, but he still managed to pummel my head a few times with his fists.

Reeling from the blows, I tried to remain focused on my own attack.

As soon as my right foot hit the ground, I lifted my left one and smacked my heel down on the man's ankle.

Meanwhile, Django tore at the other leg, his teeth sunk in deep. The man turned his attention away from me and toward my dog and started to rain blows down on Django's head to loosen the dog's death grip.

By the time my heel came down on his foot, he'd managed to strike Django's nose hard enough for my baby to yelp and pull away. That pissed me off.

I wound up for another attack when something struck me so hard I saw stars and began to fall backward. The last thing I remember was hearing Nico roaring in rage.

When I woke, I was still on the floor. Nico was holding me in his arms.

"Look at me," he said. I did and he held a flashlight to my eyes.

"Hmm."

"What?"

"I'm trying to decide if you are concussed."

I shrugged and sat up.

"How do you feel?"

"I have a headache."

He laughed. "I bet."

"Was I out for long?"

"No, thank God," he said. "A few seconds."

"Where is he?"

"Gone," Nico said. "It was chase him or check on you."

"You should've chased him."

He didn't answer.

"Rose?"

"She's fine. I texted her."

"I think we should get her. Bring her back here. If someone is after us, they might know where she is."

Nico sighed loudly. "I was thinking the same thing."

"Let's go." I stood up.

I felt a little wobbly. Nico reached for my arm.

"I will go get her. You stay here."

I swallowed. It had to be asked.

"How did that man get in here?"

Nico led me to our bedroom. There was a rope hanging outside.

"Holy fuck."

He'd rappelled down from the roof. Into our bedroom window.

"He won't be back tonight," Nico said. He pointed to the ground. There was a large pool of blood there. That's when I noticed a thick trail of blood from the hall where we had fought to this window. I leaned out. The rope fell all the way to the street below.

It sent a shudder down my spine.

Something about the man's rubber suit and silence gave me the fucking creeps.

I went to find my phone and dialed Eva.

"I'm on my way. I'll bring Rose back here. We'll call it a spontaneous vacation," she said. "But don't freak her out by grabbing her from her sleepover. I'll have someone over to watch that house within the hour. You guys sit tight. Nico should stay with you."

I agreed and hung up. Eva had connections everywhere. Rose would be safe until Eva arrived.

After, when Rose and Eva left for their "vacation," Nico and I managed to track down the attacker.

He'd had to seek treatment for the stab wound from the poker. But he had left Barcelona to do so. I had to call on an old friend to track him down.

My pal Danny in San Francisco was a world-class hacker.

He managed to narrow down exactly which hospital a man had sought treatment for a stab wound to the left side. It was across town.

Once Danny had a name, he had an address. Then he had hacked into the man's cell phone and texted us a current location—a house outside the city.

At first, Nico told me to wait at home. I just looked at him and laughed.

We waited until he went out for the night and snuck into his apartment.

When he returned, Nico was sitting there in the dark, smoking a cigarette.

"What the fuck?" the man said.

He reached for the gun in his waistband, but I was right behind him and held my own gun to his head. "Easy now, sailor."

It took a few hours with him tied to a chair, but he eventually confessed that he'd been hired on the dark web by someone calling themselves AnthraxKing. Our guy was only the hit man hired to kill us. His plan was to regroup and come back for us using Rose as bait. When I heard that, I wanted to kill him. Immediately.

Nico persuaded me to wait.

We needed to find out who had hired him.

Danny helped us do that. It turned out to be one of Nico's old enemies—a cartel boss in Mexico.

Rather than have him killed, which is what we both wanted to do, we decided to reach out to an old friend of Eva's—Detective Jay Collins in the LAPD. We gave him the cartel boss's location. He passed that on, and Nico's nemesis ended up in an American prison.

At the last minute, Nico decided not to maim our would-be assassin.

"Gia, we don't need another enemy out there," he said. "If we cut off his hands..."—which had been my idea—"he'll spend his entire life trying to get revenge."

I reluctantly agreed.

Instead, we paid him off. It wasn't how I usually did business, but it would work. I had more than my own well-being to consider. I had to think of Rose.

"And now you owe me," I told him before we left. "I may call on you one day, and I expect you to respond."

The man had nodded. He might have been a killer, but he was also apparently a man of honor.

Other than that one attack, Nico, Rose, and I lived a relatively quiet and peaceful life in Barcelona. Until the Alzheimer's appeared. Before long, I had to be the one to take charge again. Now, being in charge was my life.

I wondered if that assassin would still keep his promise if I needed to call him.

11

Down on the patio, Conner stood and held up his glass. Everyone grew quiet. I couldn't make out what he was saying, but I could tell he was making a speech, probably a toast to Lucas.

He stopped speaking and the rest of them raised their glasses and they all drank.

Suddenly, Hannah leaped up and ran away, swiping at her face with her palms.

I knew how much she hurt. I'd lost men I'd loved. Bobby. James. And now Nico.

I was so grateful for the love I'd shared with these three men.

But I knew better than to ever expect something like that again.

Deep down inside, I'd always known my destiny was to be a lone wolf.

I swallowed a lump in my throat thinking about this.

Pulling on a hoodie and baggy sweatpants over my underwear, I headed downstairs to look for Hannah.

I found her in a small sunroom off the main living room. She was sitting on a velvet love seat in the near dark, staring out the windows at nothing. I quickly stepped inside and closed the door behind me, then made my way to an armchair I could make out in the dim light streaming in the windows from the patio lights outside.

"I lost my boyfriend when I was about your age," I said and paused. She didn't say anything, but the sound of her sniffling had ceased. "He was the love of my life. But I didn't realize that until the day he was taken from me."

"Oh," she said in an emotionless voice.

"He was the only guy I ever imagined having kids with. But he was murdered right after I told him I loved him," I said and paused again.

I wondered if she would say something about the word "murdered," but she remained silent.

"And the hardest part of all was that his murder was my fault."

"What?" She said the word in a strangled voice. Guess that got her attention.

"The killer was trying to punish me."

"Oh," she said again, back to that flat monotone.

I sat there in the silence, willing her to say something, anything. It worked.

"Was he a good boyfriend?" she said in a stuffed-up voice.

"In what way?"

"Did he treat you good? Was he faithful? Did he flirt with your friends?"

Her voice was angry now. It was probably good that she was upset, but I wasn't sure.

"Yes. Yes. No."

She clamped her lips together.

"How about you answer those same questions for me," I said.

"No. No. Yes."

"Hmmm," I said.

"Right?"

"So you have mixed feelings about his death," I said. "You cared for him. But he wasn't necessarily the best boyfriend for you."

"Bingo."

I was a little surprised by this harsh side of her. It was as if the insecure, shrinking woman I'd seen the night before was gone.

"That makes his loss even tougher."

She burst into tears.

I threw my arms around her and let her sob into my embrace.

We both jumped at the sound of the door opening.

It was Conner.

"Sorry," he said in a gruff voice. "Sabine was looking for you, Hannah."

She jumped up. "Where is she?"

"In her bedroom."

Then Hannah was gone.

I stood there and let out a loud sigh.

"This must be so hard on all of you," I said.

He gave a wry grin. He had a whisky bottle in his hand. He took a slug of it and then handed it to me. I grabbed it and took my own long drink.

"Must suck for you to have all this fall into your lap."

I shrugged. I opened my mouth to speak and then shut it again. I wanted to say, what else is fucking new? But I immediately realized that it would make it seem like his friend's murder was my fault.

What I really wanted to know was who the fuck killed him? I had an idea but didn't think it was possible. I thought about the conversation I'd overheard. Was Amanda really capable of murder or was it bluster?

Conner moved closer to me. His fingers lingered on mine as he took the bottle away. His head dipped, and his mouth, hot and urgent was on mine. His body pressed against me, and I responded without thinking. It had been a long, long time since I'd felt this way.

Thank God my cell phone rang right then. We both jumped.

It was Ryder.

"Just checking on you."

"I'm fine," I'm sure I sounded annoyed.

But I was partly relieved. I didn't want to sleep with Conner. Not really.

Sabine walked in. She had on high heels and a bodycon white dress.

"We need to get out. Hannah needs to get out of this house. We're all going into town. You guys want to come?"

I paused. Yes. I needed to get out of there. I needed some air.

"I'm in," I said and walked past her. "Give me ten minutes to change."

I heard Conner behind me. "Me, too."

DOWNTOWN WAS HOPPING. The film festival kicked off the next day.

I'd nearly forgotten.

Conner, who had come with me in the Jeep, reminded me as we pulled into town behind the other vehicle with his friends in it. I sort of hated that he rode with me. It made it seem like we were a couple. Not interested.

After we parked, we walked along the promenade, scouting out clubs we might want to hit. I could have cared less, but Amanda said you couldn't be seen at the wrong club in Cannes or it might mark you for life, especially if the paparazzi caught you there and immortalized it with a photograph.

I was too stunned to respond. How could she even think this way less than twenty-four hours after her friend was murdered? Conner took my arm. "Amanda will never change. When her brother died in a car crash in high school, she still went to prom that weekend. I think it's how she protects herself. She turns her emotions on and off."

"It's pretty fucked up," I said.

He didn't respond.

Meanwhile, Hannah was decidedly not turning her emotions off. She trailed behind the group with tears streaming down her face. Sabine held her hand. That was a true friend. Not the unfeeling bitch she'd known since kindergarten. Again, I reminded myself it was none of my business.

We sat down at a sidewalk café for a quick drink "to fortify ourselves" as Owen put it. I was surprised that the three women sat together. I sat with Conner and Owen and Clint.

After a few minutes, two handsome dark-skinned men dressed in Armani and Gucci stopped at the girls' table. The men leaned over and spoke in low voices. I couldn't make out what they were saying.

Sabine shook her head, but Amanda smiled brightly. Then she must've said something about us because the men stood up to full height again and took us in. Then the taller one, who had a goatee and wore sunglasses even though it was night, nodded.

Amanda stood and came over to our table.

"We've been invited to a private party on Île Sainte-Marguerite. They'll take us there on Ahmed's yacht. Just for an hour or two. I said yes."

I raised an eyebrow. Conner looked at me. "It's an island nearby."

I drained my glass and shrugged. I was along for the ride tonight.

The last thing I wanted was to be treated as the "adult" or have the others look to me to make decisions.

THE YACHT WAS STUNNING. As yachts should be.

Besides us, there were some other women clustered on the lounge chairs toward the prow.

The night breeze felt amazing as we motored out into the dark bay. The night sky was filled with stars, and I inhaled deeply, feeling both grateful to be alive and full of sorrow for the lives I had lived and now grieved. It was bittersweet.

Conner found me and wrapped his arms around me from behind. "You were shivering," he said in my ear.

"I was?"

He didn't respond and started to kiss my neck. I turned and, still wrapped in his arms, met his mouth with mine. It was a warm, delicious kiss, but it felt wrong. I pulled back and smiled.

He looked alarmed.

"What is it?"

"Me and you? It's not going to happen."

"Did I do something?" he asked, titling his head.

"No!" I said emphatically. "You are beautiful and sexy and kind and..."

"Then what is it?"

"I don't know," I said. "I'm being totally honest and transparent with you. For some reason, it just doesn't feel right. It could be because of what I left back in Barcelona. Or maybe that's not it at all."

He gave a sweet smile. "You don't owe me an explanation."

Relief flooded me. I smiled back. "Thank you."

On the deck above, we heard angry voices and both grew quiet.

It was Owen and Amanda. They were arguing. She was crying. He sounded furious.

Conner took my hand and pulled me under the awning so we were out of sight of whomever was on the upper deck. He held a finger to his lips.

"You told me you would kill anyone I was with," Amanda said. "Did you do it? Did you kill him?"

"You admit you were cheating on me with him, then?" Owen's voice was low and deadly.

"I'm sorry."

"Too fucking late for that, Amanda."

"You didn't answer my question," she said. "I heard you arguing with him. Hannah said she heard you tell Lucas you would kill him if he was sleeping with me. Did you say that? Did you kill him? Just answer me, Owen."

Her raised voice was shrill and angry.

"Fuck you, Amanda."

Then there were footsteps stomping away over our head. Amanda's loud sobs continued above us.

Fuck.

Conner took me by the hand and led me to the side of the boat. We put our elbows on the rail, and as we looked down at the water, he swore in a whisper. "Owen killed Lucas."

I exhaled loudly. "Maybe."

"I can't believe it," he said, still whispering. "I've known both those guys my whole life. I mean we grew up playing pee-wee football together. We've wrestled and even had fist fights over girls, but when it came down to it, we always said 'bros over hoes.'"

"Classy."

"Sorry," he said. "But that's the saying."

"Yeah, I know. I have a teenage daughter."

"You do?"

"Well, adopted."

It wasn't exactly true, but whatever. Legally or not, Rose was mine.

Just then, I spotted Hannah sitting alone on a couch near a large TV screen. Nobody else was around.

"Excuse me," I said to Conner and went inside. I sat down beside her.

"Can I get you anything?"

She shook her head morosely. She was staring straight ahead at nothing.

"Hey," I said. "There's something I wanted to ask you about."

"What?" she said and turned her head to meet my eyes as if she just realized I was there.

"Did you hear Owen threaten to kill Lucas if he was sleeping with Amanda?"

I knew it was a very sensitive, loaded question, but I had to ask.

Hannah closed her eyes and nodded.

"So, it's true."

She didn't open her eyes but nodded again.

"Do you think Owen killed Lucas?"

Her eyes flew open, but she didn't answer.

Instead, she stood and walked away.

WHEN WE DOCKED at Île St. Marguerite, the others disappeared before I could get off the yacht.

Ahmed was the only one who waited for me, giving a low bow as I came up from below.

He was older, maybe in his fifties. He wore expensive jeans, leather sandals, and a white silk shirt. The neckline shone with gold necklaces. He had a large, hooked nose, dark, deep-set eyes, and a great smile, which he now flashed at me.

I couldn't help but smile back. "You are very sweet to invite us onboard and take us here," I said.

He shrugged. "I get bored easy. To have young, beautiful people around makes me happy."

I gave him another look. I wanted to tell him I knew exactly how he felt, but instead I just looped my arm through his. "Come on, captain, let's go explore."

"I will protect you," he said.

"Oooh, from what?"

I'd never heard of the island.

"This island contains the fortress prison where the Man in the Iron Mask was held in the seventeenth century."

"Huh," I said. "Never heard of the guy."

Ahmed laughed. "Some say his ghost still haunts the island. I will tell you the tale."

"Perfect," I said. "I'm in the mood for a good ghost story."

Not far from where we landed was a small village with about twenty buildings. Some looked like homes. A few were cafes.

"Should we skip the drinks and check out the prison?" I said, eyeing all the drunk young people at the sidewalk tables.

"I'm afraid you shall be disappointed in the prison," he said. "It has been turned into a youth hostel."

"Boring."

"Exactly."

Beyond the small settled area was a thick forest.

"Is the prison that way?"

Ahmed shook his head. "That is uninhabited."

"Let's go," I said.

"Why don't we go by the fort," he said. "There is a museum

there now and a cemetery next door. You should at least see it while you are here."

"Fine," I said.

As we walked, we passed a walled-off area.

"What's that?"

"Aha. That is La Grand Jardin."

"Can we go inside?"

"It was purchased recently and is now private. I have been inside though. It is quite impressive."

In moments, we were at the cemetery. I could see the fortress prison beyond the gravestones.

"Wounded French soldiers who were brought here to get well but died are buried in this cemetery," Ahmed said. "We have to wait in line. They limit visitors to keep the area nice."

I looked over and saw about ten people in line outside the big cemetery gates.

"I'm super interested in that, but let me run to the restroom first," I said.

"I will escort you," he said.

"Nah, I'm good, just save our spot in line."

The building housing the bathrooms was some ways away. When I got there, it seemed deserted but I heard a sound that sent my heart racing.

"Stop!"

It was a woman's voice. It was coming from behind the building.

"I don't want to do that," she said.

"That's not what you told me earlier."

It was Owen's voice.

"I'm going to scream," the woman said, her voice growing shrill.

I didn't wait to hear Owen's answer. I was around the corner and yanking him off the young woman, whom he had pressed up against the building. He whirled and came at me swinging. I aimed a well-placed kick on his neck and he went flying, landing with a thud on the ground.

When we turned, the woman was gone.

"You are a fucking piece of shit," I said.

"Hey, Amanda can cheat on me, so I can cheat on her."

"That's not cheating, fuckhead. That's assault."

"As soon as she told me to stop I did."

"Didn't sound that way to me," I said and glared at him, my arms crossed over my chest.

"I swear."

"I don't believe you," I said. "I don't know if you had anything to do with killing Lucas, but I promise you if you lift a finger against anyone around me, I will kill you."

"What the fuck?" he said.

Right then a group of guys came around the corner.

Owen was still on the ground, his legs out in front of him, his lip bleeding.

"Oh, sorry," one of the young men said.

"It's all good," I said. "I'm all done here."

I took the time to walk back to the cemetery to calm down. I'd have to figure out how to deal with Owen. For now, he knew better than to lift a finger against anyone when I was around.

We were reading some of the headstones when my cell rang.

It was Hannah. She was hysterical. It was difficult to make out what she said, but the gist of it was that someone had tried to kill her. She'd become separated from the group and got lost on a path leading through the thick woods. After she heard some noises, she realized someone was following her. When she turned around, the person stood there in the dark and wouldn't respond to her questions. She ran for her life, and the person chased her. Luckily, she told me, she came across a group on the path ahead. When they all turned around to confront her pursuer, they had fled.

"Did you recognize the person?"

"No," she said. "I couldn't tell if it was a man or woman."

"Where are you now?"

"I walked with this group back to the prison."

I looked around. Then I saw her. She was sitting on a small wall with her legs casually crossed, swinging her feet. She didn't look traumatized. Good.

"We're here."

I hung up and turned to Ahmed. "Hate to be a spoil sport, but I think we need to leave the island."

After everyone was rounded up to get back on the yacht, people crowded around Hannah to ask her what happened.

Nobody asked about Owen and where he was.

I stood nearby, trying to act casual, but watched everyone's faces and postures closely. Especially Owen's. He stood in the back by the bar, pouring and downing shot after shot.

Sabine sat with her arm around Hannah, rubbing her back.

"I don't know what happened," she said. "One minute you were with us, and the next, when I turned around, you were gone."

Hannah blinked. "Yeah. I stopped to read this placard, and think I ended up taking the wrong path."

Amanda sat on the couch across from Hannah with a strange look on her face.

Things were obviously still very frosty between the two friends.

Owen came over and handed Amanda a tumbler of golden liquid, which she downed. And then she leaned forward with her elbows on her thighs, staring at Hannah.

"What?" Hannah said. "Just fucking say it."

"Seems strange that you were the only one attacked tonight."

I swiveled my head toward Owen. His face had grown sheet white.

"What do you mean?"

"Just seems a little coincidental that you got lost and you got attacked."

Sabine glanced at both women's faces, clearly worried.

She cleared her throat and said, "Well, I guess Amanda got lost too."

"You did?" Hannah said, and her eyes narrowed.

Amanda shrugged. "Only for a few minutes."

"Oh, how fucking convenient," Hannah said. "You disappeared at the exact same time that I was attacked?"

I waited, but nobody mentioned Owen leaving the group. What the hell?

At this point, Amanda had leaped out of her seat and was clawing at Hannah before anyone could react. She screamed, "How dare you? How dare you accuse me? You act like Miss Fucking Innocent, but we both know differently, don't we?"

Hannah was fighting back. "You shut the fuck up if you know what's good for you."

Some idiots also onboard were yelling, "Cat fight."

Sabine and Conner rushed in and broke up the fight, each taking one woman off to the side.

I looked over at Owen. He was slumped at a bar stool looking into his drink.

12

Back on the yacht, I pretended to guess how old they were then feigned disbelief until they showed me their licenses to prove it. Armed with their full names and dates of birth, I called Danny in San Francisco.

"I need everything you can dig up on these two women," I said and reeled off Amanda and Hannah's information. I also gave him Owen's first and last name, saying all I knew is that he was from L.A.

"I know it's not much but anything you can find would help."

Danny said he'd get back to me in a few hours. He was away from home right then.

"What?"

This was welcome news.

He cleared his throat. Was he embarrassed?

"I'm, uh, well, my girlfriend and I, we started walking every day, and we're on a walk."

"That fantastic, Danny."

I worried about that kid so much. He had a disease called gigantism where he grew too much and too fast and might die young. But I tried to never think about that last aspect of it.

Danny finding a girlfriend a few years back was the best thing ever. She was a good influence and took care of him, making him eat real food like fruits and vegetables instead of endless boxes of pizza. Now, she was making him walk. I could not be happier.

"Take your time, D," I said. "And tell Rachel hello for me."

I hung up.

From the kitchen window, I could see that Sabine, Clint, and Conner were out at the pool. For a second that worried me. But I figured Amanda and Owen were probably in their room and Hannah, hopefully, was in hers. Keeping those two women apart was key right now.

I had just headed outside when my phone rang.

It was Commissaire Boucher. I'd given him my number when he interviewed me. I pivoted away from the pool area and went off to a small garden on the side of the house.

"We will be there in the morning to make an arrest."

"Keep talking," I said.

He paused as if waiting for me to say something more.

My heart beat double-time. I closed my eyes. This couldn't be happening.

Calm the fuck down, Santella. Think. He remained silent, obviously waiting for me to speak first. I inhaled sharply.

"I'm assuming it's not me you're going to arrest, or you wouldn't have called first," I said.

"Very astute," he said.

"Is that sarcasm?"

He gave a small chuckle. "We will be taking Amanda into custody. Based on your statement and some other interesting evidence."

I frowned. "With all due respect, I don't think she has it in her," I said. "If you're arresting her just based on what I overheard, please rethink this. I can't imagine her doing it."

"That's what I thought at first, as well," he admitted. "Which is why the arrest has been so delayed, but ultimately I cannot argue with the evidence."

"Why are you telling me all this?" I said.

"Ryder vouched for you."

"Huh." I wondered again what his connection with the police department was.

"I want you to be aware of the situation to keep yourself safe."

"You don't have to worry about me," I said. "But I don't understand. What else makes you think it's Amanda?"

He sighed.

"Blood on some of her clothing. In her suitcase, we found a supply of a drug we suspect will come back in Lucas's toxicology report," he said. "We also drew blood from Hannah. We think both of them were drugged. I will see you in the morning. I suggest you lock the door to your room tonight."

"Like I said, you don't have to worry about me, but I still have a hard time believing that Amanda is a killer."

"Goodnight," he said and hung up.

I walked back toward the door leading into the house. As I did, I saw a figure on one of the balconies upstairs melt into the dark shadows. I strained my eyes but couldn't see anyone. Someone had been eavesdropping. The balcony was a public one off of a sitting room upstairs. One that anyone could have accessed.

I would be keeping Ryder's gun close tonight.

IN ADDITION to locking my bedroom doors, I set an expensive-looking vase on the floor against it, hoping the sound of it shattering or, at the very least, falling over, would wake me if someone managed to unlock my door. I stuck Ryder's gun on the nightstand and crawled under the covers, leaving the French doors open to the balcony.

It would take someone with the superpowers of Spiderman to get onto my balcony. Or...someone with a ladder. Thinking this, I got out of bed and closed the doors, irritated that I'd lost the cool night breeze.

I didn't think anyone in the house had the balls to confront me, but who knew? Plus, honestly, despite the detective's confidence in his evidence, I had a hell of a hard time believing anyone in the house, especially Amanda, could kill anyone.

If so, she was a damn good actress.

If I had to pick one of them, my money would've been on Owen.

I reached over and felt for my phone and called the detective. It went straight to voicemail.

I opened my mouth to leave a message, but then didn't know what to say. What could I say? I thought that Lucas and Amanda were having an affair and that Owen killed his competition?

I hung up. Maybe I would try to have a conversation with the detective in person the next day.

Even through my closed window I could hear the others out at the pool until late, talking. Even knowing one of them might be a killer, the murmur of their voices was strangely soothing. I'd obviously been alone too long.

Finally, my mind settled from all the possible scenarios and thoughts of murder, and I fell asleep.

When I woke, the house was silent, and the sun was just starting to flood my bedroom. The first thing I did was throw open the French Doors and go stand out at the balcony rail, looking down on the pool.

There were no bodies floating in it this morning.

The others had cleaned up any remnants of their occupancy

from the night before. Towels were neatly folded on a lawn chair. No empty cups or bottles. No trash. Even the ashtrays were emptied.

For some reason, I felt uneasy.

The police would be here soon to arrest Amanda.

But was she guilty?

I took a quick shower, pulled on some baggy sweatpants and a tiny camisole top, and headed downstairs to make some coffee. Not for the first time, I regretted not staying in a hotel where I could order room service.

I walked past the other bedrooms on my way to the stairs. All the doors were shut.

Downstairs, I jumped and nearly screamed when I passed by Owen sprawled in a big leather armchair in the living room. I froze until I heard him snore loudly.

A bottle of some brown alcohol lay on the Persian rug at his feet. His head was thrown back and his mouth was wide open. Even so, he was sort of sweet-looking in sleep. But he might have killed Lucas. Had Amanda suspected it and kicked him out of her bed last night, sending him to drink himself into a stupor down here?

In the kitchen, I grabbed a large chef's knife and put it on the counter between me and the entrance to the living room, just in case. I wasn't afraid of him. But I also didn't really trust anyone in the house at this point. Might as well anticipate any possible scenario. It was what a warrior would do. It had been much too long since I had to think like that.

Even the last attack on my family had been handled by Rose.

A lunatic had gone after Nico, and Rose had taken her down.

Thinking of Rose made my heart suddenly clench. I missed that girl more than I could say. It seemed like every minute, she was drawing further and further away from me. The more intent

she became on finding and killing her enemy, the less she wanted to do with me.

On some level I understood. It hurt her too much to have a close relationship with me. I'd been there. I got it on a deep level. But that didn't mean I had to like it.

Once Nico no longer recognized her, she'd fled.

I was lucky if she responded to my calls and texts once every two months.

As I thought all of this, I ground the beans for the coffee while the hot water heated in a kettle on the stove. I glanced into the living room to see if all the commotion had woken Owen. But his head was still thrown back, and his eyes were closed.

Soon, the water was ready, and I poured it into the French press. I pushed down slowly at first but then impatiently plunged it all the way and poured my first cup, which was about half the pot. I missed my Moka pot, but this still made a damn good cup of coffee.

Taking my coffee cup and the French press pot, I slipped out the back door and settled into a chair near the pool, watching as the sun poured over the edge of the tall wall and lit up the white marble patio and backyard.

I knew I should enjoy the peace before all hell broke loose. I wondered when the detective was going to arrive with his dark news and arrest warrant.

I finished my first cup, dusted off the second, and then headed back into the kitchen. I dumped the cup and pot and walked past Owen again. Out cold. Still.

Upstairs, I was suddenly compelled to talk to Amanda. I didn't know why. I just honestly didn't think she was a killer. I wanted to hear what she had to say before the detective arrived. Maybe, just maybe, if she convinced me she was innocent, I could intervene before her arrest.

I knocked softly on her door. As I did, it slowly swung open a few inches.

"Amanda?" I said in a low voice.

There was no answer.

"Amanda?" I said again. Then I pushed my head inside. I saw a leg. Where it shouldn't be: on the floor. I stepped all the way inside. It only took a quick glance to see the plume of blood that flared out on the carpet around Amanda's midsection. She was face down, her head turned away from me. She wore tiny athletic shorts and a T-shirt that was pushed part way up her back. As I drew closer, I saw her face. It was a ghastly color. Even so, I raced over and knelt down to check for a pulse I knew wouldn't be there.

13

Standing in the doorway of Amanda's room, I dialed Commissaire Boucher.

He answered on the first ring.

"Bad news."

There was a sharp intake of breath and then he asked, "Who?"

"Amanda." I said the name in a whisper because I'd heard some noise downstairs.

"I'm on my way."

I hung up and turned to see Owen standing there behind me.

"Jesus," I said, startled.

He was holding a butcher knife down by his side.

His eyes grew wide when he saw me take in the knife.

He started to say something, but I'd already wound up and kicked his wrist. The knife clattered to the floor, but I wasn't done. I yanked his arm and twisted it, bringing him to his knees, and then jutted my knee up into his solar plexus.

Then he was on the ground, and I was on his back while he moaned.

"You got it wrong," he gasped out.

"Oh, yeah? Why did you come at me with a knife?"

"I heard something upstairs and grabbed the knife in case it was an intruder."

"Really?" I said sarcastically.

"Swear to God."

I lifted my knee off his back.

Then I leaped off of him and stood a few feet away, kicking the knife further down the hall behind me before I whirled to face him again. I watched as he pulled himself to his feet. I stood with my legs wide, staring at him and leaning forward in case I had to attack again.

"Amanda is dead," I said, without preamble.

His mouth dropped open in shock.

He hadn't known.

"What? How?" He turned toward the bedroom door.

"Stay here," I said. "The detective is on his way to process the scene."

"I need to see her," he said in a choked voice. I shook my head.

"Not gonna happen."

"You can't stop me," he shouted in a strangled voice and charged me.

At first, I got ready to do a throat stab, but I didn't want to really hurt him, so I went with a temple punch. He slumped to the ground.

I looked up to see that the noise had brought everyone out in the hall.

I stood there over Owen's body panting, my hair flopping in my eyes.

"I'm sorry," I said. "Amanda's dead. The detective is on his way. I need someone to let them in while I make sure nobody else goes into Amanda's room."

Sabine's face grew sheet white, then she burst into tears.

"I can't take it anymore. I can't. I just can't. I want to go home," she said.

Hannah just stared at me for a long moment and then abruptly turned around, marched into her room, and slammed the door. I heard the deadbolt slide shut.

Conner was at my side. "Are you okay?" he looked down at Owen, who was moaning and starting to stir.

"I had to stop him from going in there," I said, jutting my chin toward the room where Amanda's body was. "He wouldn't listen. He should be okay in a few minutes."

I felt guilty for knocking him out, but not that guilty.

Kneeling down, Conner helped Owen sit up. "You okay, buddy?"

"Will you take him to your room and maybe lock the door?" I asked.

He looked at me and frowned at first but then nodded. "Sure."

Owen finally noticed me and glared. "You're a crazy bitch."

"You have no idea," I said. Conner led Owen to his room, and I waited until the door closed.

Then I looked over at Sabine and Clint. "Why don't the two of you go to your rooms, as well. I think everyone should just stay locked in their rooms until the detective arrives."

Sabine looked at me, tears streaming down her face. "Someone is killing us one-by-one."

I didn't respond.

She wasn't wrong.

Once I was alone, I glanced at Amanda's door.

I wasn't sure how to lock it from the outside, but I would figure out a way to make it hard for someone to sneak in undetected. There was a large bureau at the end of the hall that held candles and extra bedding. I pushed it over in front of her door.

It made a loud screeching noise and was probably scratching the beautiful wooden floor. At this point, I didn't give a shit. I figured getting any deposit back was ludicrous. I was surprised the owners hadn't heard about the murders already and come to kick us all out.

Once the bureau was in place, I felt comfortable going back downstairs. Anyone would be able scoot it aside, but it would be an obnoxiously loud process that I would hear.

I went to the front door, disarmed the alarm, and propped the door wide open. Then I went into the kitchen and started the kettle. I was going to need some coffee to get through this morning.

As soon as the water was boiling, I made another French press pot of coffee. I poured a cup and headed back toward the stairs. I sat at the top of the stairs on the landing with my back to the wall that once held the bureau and waited for the detective and his crew to arrive.

I was about half way through my cup when I thought to call Ryder.

"I'm on my way."

"One of these days you're going to have to tell me your hook-up with the police department here."

He sighed.

"Is it bad?"

No answer.

"Are you really a cop? Private eye? Career criminal working as an informant? Spill it, sailor."

"Boucher is my brother-in-law."

"You have a sister?"

"No."

"Oh."

He was married. For some ridiculous fucking reason, I found this disappointing.

"You're married?"

I found I was holding my breath waiting for him to answer.

When he answered, it was in a very quiet voice. "No."

"So he's your ex brother-in-law?"

"I guess."

"Huh."

"I was married to his sister."

His responses were very confusing. I didn't get it.

"But you're not married to her anymore?"

The silence seemed to stretch on, and I suddenly got an inkling of what he was about to say. Horror shot through me. But it was too late.

"She is dead."

"I'm so sorry."

Then he hung up.

I stared at my phone. Fuck. Way to be an insensitive prick, Santella. I pushed him and pushed him until he said it. And all for what?

That last question was one I wasn't ready to answer. Not right then. I wasn't about to admit to myself why I was so eager to find out if he was married or not.

TWENTY MINUTES LATER, I heard someone downstairs.

"Hello?"

It was the detective.

He was followed by three officers. He made his way up the stairs, and I stood, stretching.

"I had a tough time keeping her boyfriend, Owen, away," I said. "We sort of got into a fight, and I knocked him out. I told them all to stay in their rooms until you got here. I had him go in someone else's room in the meantime."

"I'm assuming this is her room?"

The detective stood in front of the bureau. He nodded, and the men with him lifted the dresser and moved it to one side.

He pulled on gloves and reached for the door handle. I swallowed, knowing what he was about to find inside. He entered, two of the men followed him and then the door shut, leaving me and one of his officers in the hall staring awkwardly at one another.

"Do you want a cup of coffee?" I asked.

The officer shook his head. Didn't even crack a smile.

"Okay. I'll be in my room if the commissaire needs me," I said.

I was relieved to be off guard duty and quickly went down the hall to my own room.

Once inside, I slid the deadbolt and flopped into bed.

I squeezed my eyes shut tightly. I had a pretty good idea who the murderer was.

But I didn't think the detective thought the same thing.

I went into the bathroom to shower and dress in something more presentable than short shorts and a tank top.

Digging into my suitcase, I found a cute orange sundress and threw that on before I made my way back downstairs. The door to Amanda's room was still closed, and the officer still stood guard in front of it, so I was surprised to see the detective in the kitchen talking to Ryder.

For some reason I was embarrassed to see them together. Probably because now, thanks to my prying, I knew what their relationship stemmed from.

They drew apart when I entered the kitchen.

"We have made an arrest," Boucher said.

Owen was in custody for killing Lucas and Amanda.

The hand pouring my coffee froze in mid-air.

"Really?" I said without turning to face them.

"It was a sordid love triangle."

The detective said that Lucas had drowned after being hit in the head by Owen and that Amanda had been shot to death. With my gun, it appeared. The gun had been found in Owen and Amanda's room during the initial search.

"It seems certain it was the murder weapon," Boucher said. "There were no fingerprints on the gun."

He was watching my face very carefully.

"Really?" I said. "Not even mine? That's odd." And should make me a suspect.

"You seem surprised."

I turned before he could read the expression on my face.

"You have a lot of evidence indicating it's Owen?"

"Enough."

That was a strange answer. I turned back around. Boucher was looking at Ryder. But when I turned my attention toward him, he looked away and wouldn't meet my eyes. What the hell?

There was some commotion by the door, and both men exchanged a look. "The coroner is here to retrieve the body."

"What about contacting the ambassador? Lucas was just sitting here for hours." It was crude, but true.

The detective sighed loudly. "It is sad, but now that we just went through the process, we know how to do it more quickly. I will tell the others to remain in their rooms. We have already taken Owen into custody. As soon as we leave, you may tell them to come out."

"Me?"

He frowned.

"Okay, fine," I said.

I wondered where Conner was. I also wondered how they had arrested Owen so quietly without me hearing him protest. I couldn't imagine he wouldn't have screamed and shouted and fought them tooth-and-nail.

But instead, I watched them walk to the door and greet the coroner and his staff.

I wasn't interested in seeing them carry Amanda's body down the stairs. It was just too damn sad. I took my coffee cup and went to sit out at the pool. As I settled into a lawn chair, I looked up at the balconies facing the pool. There was mine. Next was Conner's room. Then Hannah's and then Amanda's and on the far end, Sabine and Clint's. As my eyes flickered over Hannah's balcony, the curtain fluttered. I didn't know if it was a breeze or if she was watching me. A few seconds later, Conner was out on his balcony. He leaned over the edge, his elbows on the railing, and lit a joint before he glanced over and saw me.

I lifted a hand to greet him, and he gave me a slight nod.

We stared at each other for a few seconds before I turned away and leaned back in the lounge chair. I closed my eyes, letting the morning sun beat on my face.

Some vacation.

Now all I wanted to do was escape from this luxurious villa and these people.

But I knew it wasn't over yet.

14

CONNER WAS ESCORTING HANNAH TO THE FILM FESTIVAL.

I didn't ask, but I overheard them discussing it.

We'd been basically stuck in the house for three days while they continued to investigate both murders.

Hannah was sobbing and Conner was speaking to her in a low soothing voice.

"Hannah, you need to go. I need to go. We need get out of this house or I'm going to go crazy. You have to go. Amanda would have wanted you to go."

"I was so awful to her," Hannah said. "I'll never forgive myself."

I paused and despite myself kept listening.

"Listen, we all know Amanda was difficult. She was terrible and beautiful and fucking irresistible."

There was a loud sniff.

"And you were a wonderful friend to her, but she could've been a better friend to you, right?"

"Maybe."

"And Lucas, he was a good guy, but he could've been a better boyfriend to you."

Another sniff.

"I miss them both, too. I'm sad as fuck, too. But I think you should go. I've thought about it a lot. I don't think it's disrespectful to them or their memories."

"You don't?"

Conner was quiet for a few seconds.

"No," he finally said. "I think we should go. Go put on that red dress you bought and I'll meet you by the door in an hour. I'll talk to Gia about taking the Rolls. It will be good for us to get out of the house. I promise."

I couldn't hear Hannah's response, but heard footsteps.

A few seconds later, Conner was bounding down the stairs. He jumped, startled when he saw me at the bottom.

"Hey, I'm taking Hannah to the festival. I think it'll be good for her. We're going early. She has tickets to some pre-showing party with Coppola."

I nodded and smiled. "Sounds cool. Want to take the Rolls?"

"Yeah," he said, scratching his head. "That's what I was going to ask."

"Of course. Have fun. The keys are on the hook in the kitchen."

He gave me a sweet smile and my heart melted a little. Then he paused and tilted his head.

"Don't," I said.

He shrugged. "A guy can try, right?"

He grew closer and reached up to tuck my hair behind my ear. I felt myself drawn to him. I swallowed the lump that was suddenly in my throat. He moved in to kiss me and I sidestepped, grabbing his wrist gently. I leaned over to his ear and whispered,

"You're a great guy, Conner."

Then I walked past him, proud of my self control.

Sabine and Clint came downstairs and said they'd called a car to take them to the train station. Clint was heading to Paris. They were going to have a late dinner and he was catching a midnight train and then Sabine would hire a driver to bring her back here.

I didn't ask why the plans had changed. Once again, it was none of my business.

After everyone left, I grabbed a bottle of white wine and retreated to my bedroom.

I slid the deadbolt and stripped naked.

In the bathroom, I ran the water as hot as I could into the large Jacuzzi tub.

Bubbles were nearly overflowing the tub and I'd just poured a glass of wine and was about to get into the water when my phone rang in the bedroom.

I rushed into the other room, wondering, as always, if it would be Rose or a nurse calling about Nico.

It was Ryder.

"I'll be there at four," he said.

"Excuse me?"

"I'm escorting you to the festival. You have tickets, right?"

I did. They were electronic tickets on my phone. I'd received a reminder about them earlier.

"Maybe."

"I think we should go. I'm your escort. I know you might find this hard to believe, but I clean up okay and do own a tux. I'll be there in an hour."

And then he hung up before I answered. I stared at my phone. How cocky! Arrogant!

I tossed the phone across the bed.

I had plans for a long bath and then I was going to crawl into bed and read a book until I couldn't keep my eyes open. This was the first night in days I had the entire villa to myself.

Despite all of this, I felt a slight tremor of excitement. The festival might be fun.

And it probably would be good for me to get out of the villa. The entire place had a pall about it. It wasn't just the recent murders. And it wasn't a pall that existed before I arrived. It was something else. If I didn't know better I would say that the dark shadows of my past—all the grief I still carried around with me—were flitting around my peripheral vision at every turn.

Maybe Ryder was right.

Sitting home alone tonight suddenly seemed depressing and slightly creepy.

Inside the walk-in closet, I unzipped the garment bag containing the dress Dante had chosen for me. I trailed my fingers across the dark green silk. It was gorgeous. It was Celine. It was sleeveless and had a very low cut neckline, nearly to my abdomen, but was structured so that there was barely any cleavage to be seen. It hugged my hips and legs to the ground. I wasn't into flouncy, puffy skirts. It would do perfectly. A black faux fur wrap was on another hanger to bring in case it was chilly inside the theaters. There was another bag with the black patent leather Christian Louboutin pumps with the four-inch-heels.

Dante had also packed dangling emerald earrings.

With everything laid out on the bed, I realized I didn't need to think about anything. Dante had done it all. The only thing I needed to do was bathe and then put on some dark eyeliner and lipstick and dress. My hair would be brushed out and could hang down my back. It was freshly washed and didn't look too ragged yet.

Sometimes having a super stylish gay best friend was the best thing ever.

Despite myself, as I slipped into the bath and sipped my

wine, I started to get a little bit excited about what the night would hold.

I told myself it had absolutely nothing to do with spending more time with Ryder. In a tuxedo.

THE RED CARPET was a blur of bright flashes as the paparazzi snapped photos of Ryder and me, wondering the whole time who we were, I'm sure. Pulling up in the Maserati that had been parked in the garage had caught their eye, apparently.

Inside, we found our seats and settled in for the first film. It was good, but I soon grew antsy and told Ryder I wanted to go have a smoke.

We grabbed flutes of champagne and headed off to an enclosed garden area where others had snuck off to spark cigarettes and joints.

Ryder led me to a small bench near some Jasmine bushes and lit my joint for me, taking a puff first. He exhaled with his eyes slightly closed, which I found extremely sexy for some reason.

"I haven't smoked marijuana in years."

"Really?"

"It was used as a treatment for my wife's cancer."

His face seemed to close up then and his body slightly turned away. I placed my hand on his. "I'm sorry to pry."

Then he turned toward me and fixed me with such an intense gaze I nearly gasped.

"I haven't really spoken about her to very many people," he said. "I would say it's still fresh, but it's not. It's been three years."

"I'm very sorry," I said.

"She was very kind and gentle," he said. "The opposite of me. She was a school teacher. Her whole life revolved around children and the bitter irony was that she could not conceive. Her first bout of cancer was when she was young and they took all those parts out to save her life. She always said it was worth it to live and meet me. But then it came back."

He looked down. I squeezed his hand and he continued.

"When she went to the cancer ward to get her treatments they said she lit up the entire place. Her whole goal during her last days was to make everyone else okay. She was kind and wouldn't hurt a soul. I've never met anyone as generous and loving and giving as she was."

He sobbed as he spoke.

I waited a few seconds and then said, "She was obviously an incredible blessing to everyone who knew her."

He drew back and looked at me. "Yes. That's it."

We stood to go back inside and I couldn't help but think that he couldn't have described a woman who was more opposite than me.

15

After we all got home, Ryder offered to make us nightcaps. While he made our drinks, I'd run upstairs and changed into baggy shorts and a cropped top before coming back down to the pool.

Conner sat on the end of my lounge chair and trailed his finger down my bare leg. I jerked away and then felt guilty. I couldn't tell if it was because of the startled, hurt look on Conner's face or the way Ryder quickly looked away when I glanced over at him. He was sitting near the others across the pool.

Fuck.

Without looking our way, Ryder stood up and headed into the house.

I stood and followed. I was a little unsteady and realized that I was drunk.

Ryder wasn't in the kitchen.

I found him in a small sunroom on the main floor. It had floor to ceiling windows and had an astonishing view of the bay with the moon rising over it. The entire room was lit up nearly as bright as day in a blueish glow from the moonlight.

I wasn't sure how I'd missed this room before.

"Hey, sailor," I said, to try to lighten the mood.

He looked at me and gave me that squinty smile. His teeth were brilliant white and I found myself mesmerized by them until he turned back to the view.

"It's so ethereal," I said walking over to stand beside him.

Standing that close, I could smell his cologne. And something else, darker, primal. He turned slightly toward me and his arm brushed mine sending an electric charge through me. With that simple touch, I was suddenly overcome with desire for Ryder.

It was ridiculous.

I held my glass up to him in a salute, swirling the melting ice in the amber liquid at the bottom of it.

"Where can a gal get a refill around here?"

"Don't you think maybe you've had enough?"

I scoffed. "Hardly."

I stood and stretched languidly. As I did, my top rode up, exposing my stomach.

His eyes flickered over me slowly. I held my breath and couldn't look away from his mouth. When his eyes rose to meet mine, heat spread throughout my core. I couldn't even remember the last time a man looked at me in that way. Even sweet and sexy Conner hadn't looked at me like that. Finally, I broke eye contact.

"So no drink?"

He shook his head.

"Don't judge me, sailor," I said. "I think finding two dead bodies in the space of two days might warrant a little overindulging."

He laughed.

I frowned. "What?"

"Please," he said.

My mouth was wide open.

"Don't act like you're traumatized by dead bodies, Gia."

"What are you talking about?"

"You forget how we know each other."

Oh. Yeah. Dante probably told him my whole fucking life story.

I backed up, staring at him with my eyes narrowed.

"You aren't some damsel in distress, so drop the fucking offended and traumatized princess act."

Instead of giving in to my desire to punch him, I trailed my fingers down his tattoo. His entire body reacted. A tremor ran through him, and he dipped his head into his shoulder. I could see his jaw clench. He was fighting for self-control. Good.

I leaned down and whispered in his ear. "So what am I then?"

He grabbed my wrist, and I gasped.

His mouth was hot near my ear. "You are the same as me."

"Oh yeah? And what is that?"

"A killer."

I yanked my arm away and headed back outside where everyone else was, my face flushed.

But Ryder never came back out. I waited about thirty minutes and then went to the front of the house and looked out the window. His car was gone, too.

Damn it.

16

WHEN I GOT DOWNSTAIRS THE NEXT MORNING, THE GROUP IN THE living room turned as one toward me. They looked so serious. I quickly scanned to see who was missing because they sure looked like they'd found another dead body. There were only the two of them: Conner and Sabine.

"Where's Hannah?"

"She's gone," Sabine said and sniffed.

I stared. Was this a euphemism for "murdered?"

Conner saw me pause.

"She took the car. We don't know when or where she went."

Relief filled me. I didn't think I could handle another dead person under my watch. I realized that I hadn't set the alarm last night after Ryder left.

"I think we need to go look for her," I said.

Conner walked toward me, but I quickly deflected his advance. "Why don't the three of you take the Rolls. You can drive, Conner," I said. "Maybe head down to the harbor and promenade and split up from there. If she left last night, maybe she went to the clubs. We should show people her picture and see if anyone saw her."

"Um, okay," he said, seeming disappointed, but I also noted that he didn't mind me handing him the keys to the convertible Rolls Royce.

I had an idea where Hannah might be, but I wanted to confront her alone. It was my best chance of saving her.

I'd figured out the night before that she was the killer.

After Ryder left, Danny had emailed me some interesting information.

Hannah had been the only survivor in a bizarre accident that had taken the lives of her mother, father, and baby sister. She claimed to have gotten up in the middle of the night, hungry for a midnight snack. She decided on grilled cheese and turned the stove on, but then claimed to have sleepwalked her dog in the middle of the night. The house filled with gas and later exploded.

I'd stayed up late thinking.

Too many things didn't add up.

I replayed every interaction I'd had with Hannah from the moment we'd met.

One thing that stuck out was that she'd known Lucas had hit his head before ending up in the pool. Even though she'd never seen the body. That first morning she'd said, "It was an accident. He must have had too much to drink, hit his head, and fell in the pool and drowned."

She said this without seeing the body or the blood.

In addition, it seemed odd that she had been pursued by someone on the island. It had likely been a story to deflect suspicion. Same with the story about her overhearing Owen threaten to kill Lucas.

She could easily have put the drug into Lucas's drink and then had some of the drug put in her water later after she killed him. Too many things didn't add up.

I could only come to one conclusion: Hannah had killed both Lucas and Amanda.

I planned to take Hannah aside, maybe on a drive today, and get her to confess.

But she had made that a little tougher by disappearing.

I had a good idea where she might be. And it was not ideal.

It was a place that she'd only go if she wanted to end it in a different way.

TWO HOURS LATER, I pulled into Cassis, just south of Marseille.

I was less interested in its quaint village setting and more interested in the limestone cliffs. La Ciotat as they were called, were the highest seaside cliffs in Europe. They had been a landmark to sailors for centuries. The area, according to Hannah, was also the setting for the world's first motion picture shown in public: *L'Arrivée d'un train en gare de La Ciotat*, a fifty-second film that premiered in Paris in 1895.

Hannah had spoken so passionately about this area the first night we met.

The significance of this location to her could not be understated.

She'd also mentioned another reason for wanting to visit here: It was where the movie *A Deadly Union* had been filmed.

When I asked her about the movie, she'd given me a brief synopsis. I'd forgotten most of it except that in one of the most dramatic scenes, a new bride is found dead at the base of the cliffs.

If my hunch was right, the cliffs were where I'd find Hannah.

I only hoped I'd find her in time and she'd still be on top of the cliffs—not at the bottom.

After I drove through town, I found the road leading to the

cliffs. As I came up on them, I saw the Chevy Tahoe parked on the shoulder of the road.

I found Hannah standing on the edge of the cliff, facing the sun. I snuck a glance over the side as I walked over to her. The water was hundreds of feet below. As I glanced down, I saw there was no chance she could land in the turquoise water below and survive. Not at that height. And it was much more likely she'd end up on the rocky outcropping at the bottom where the surf was breaking. Or, if she didn't fall out far enough, she would strike the jagged cliffside all the long way down.

The odds weren't good any way you looked at it. It wasn't a chance I would take.

She was wearing a loose maxi dress billowing in the wind. My first thought was that if she tried to move, she would probably trip on its hem, and she would fall. She was also wearing high-heeled wedge sandals with the toes overhanging the edge of the rock. If she shifted slightly, she would also tumble over the edge.

I tried not to show alarm.

As if she sensed me coming, she turned. I braced for her to lose her balance and fall but only her head swiveled. The rest of her continued to face the sea.

"It's you."

I gave a small shrug.

"Where are the police?"

"Why would they be here?"

"Because I killed people!"

"Oh," I said. "Want to talk about it?"

I was trying to keep her talking while I figured out a way to get her away from the edge of the cliff. The rocks she was standing on did not look very sturdy or secure. I took a few steps closer.

"Back up. If you don't, I swear I'll jump right now." Spittle flew out of her mouth. Her eyes were wild.

"Listen, I just want to talk."

She shook her head. "You think I'm a freak, a monster."

"You think you're the only one who has killed someone?" I gave a small laugh. "I've killed quite a few times, in fact. I've actually lost track of how many people I've killed. Definitely more than two, though."

Her eyes narrowed now.

"Why are you telling me this?" she asked.

She shifted, and a pebble under her foot loosened and plunged to the rocks below.

"Just so you know that anything can be fixed. Even when it seems like it's all over, it can get better. I promise."

Now she glared at me. "What game are you playing?"

"I'm not playing a game, Hannah," I said, now meeting her eyes straight on. "I just think that you need some help."

"Fuck you," she said.

"I don't think you're a killer."

Her lower lip began to tremble and then a flood of tears rolled down her face.

"Well, I've killed more than two people, too." She had a smug look on her face.

"Do you mean your family?" I said in a soft voice.

Her face crumpled. "Yes. But they deserved to die. They didn't like me. They hated me."

"Okay," I said in a matter-of-fact voice.

"But there was someone else."

"Really?" I said, genuine interest in my voice.

"Amanda is the only one who knew. That's why she had to die."

I remembered the conversation I'd overheard between Lucas and Amanda.

"I'm not going to wait much longer," she said.

This time I heard him answer. "Be patient."

"If it doesn't happen tonight, it's over. I'll do it myself."

"She'll know it was you. You'll ruin everything."

"Don't you push me. Don't you tempt me. You have no idea what I'm capable of."

"I'm not afraid of you," he said.

"You should be."

It sounded like they were going to go to the police.

"Who was that?" I asked.

"This girl who liked Lucas. They had sex when Amanda and Lucas were dating. That's why they broke up. Amanda found out about it because of me. And then I killed the girl."

"How?"

"She was drunk and I pushed her off this bridge we were on."

"Why didn't you kill Amanda when she was dating him?"

"Because she was my best friend, duh?"

"So, why did you kill her now?"

"She was going to go to the police. She told me."

"I have a question. If you loved Lucas, why did you kill him?"

"It was an accident. We got in a fight. I drugged him. But I didn't mean for it to kill him. Or maybe I did. We argued, I pushed him. He hit his head and fell in the pool. He might have still been alive. But I didn't get help. I don't know why. Maybe because he was sleeping with Amanda. Maybe because I just wanted him dead." She shook her head. "I don't know anymore."

It was a lie. A good one, that I think she actually convinced herself to believe.

"But I needed to kill Amanda. I didn't want to. I needed to. I used your gun to frame you."

"I know."

"Now I have nobody," she said. "Now I want to die."

Fuck. This was not where I wanted this conversation to go.

"Hannah, I need you to come over here and talk about this with me. I know how you feel. I've killed people before and regretted it. It's not a great feeling. But it gets better. I promise."

"I'm not you."

"True. But we might be more alike than you realize."

I was starting to panic. She was inching closer to the edge.

"Bullshit," she said. "You're fucking perfect. You have the perfect life. You are confident, beautiful, strong, and in charge all the time."

"Not true."

She made a face.

I swallowed.

"I never wanted to kill someone," I said.

But I hadn't been given a choice. Not really.

After I was raped in my late teens, it seemed inevitable that my attacker would die by my hands. The next person I killed really forced my hand. Literally.

It was his death that spawned a chain of events that would change my life forever.

Mateo Antonio Turricci. That green-eyed Sicilian devil. He'd killed my parents, my godfather, and maybe my brother. He was a monster. I didn't know about him until long after my parent's death. Then I learned that when my mother was orphaned as a child in Sicily, he had become her guardian. When she was a teen, he'd raped her. She'd managed to escape to America and carve out a new life for herself.

But he remained obsessed with her. For decades.

Shortly after I moved away from home, he killed my mother and father, thinking I was his child and my mother had never told him. When I found out later, I hunted him down to kill him.

Even though I am American-born, my Sicilian roots require me to exact vengeance on those who kill my loved ones.

When I found him, I showed him proof that I wasn't his daughter right before the police arrived. Faced with this knowledge, he threw himself on the fireplace poker I was holding. As it slid into his chest and the life left his body, I saw in his eyes that he died with the realization that I wasn't his daughter after all.

Later, his children came to kill me.

His daughter failed. And died.

His son took my boyfriend, Bobby's, life before I managed to kill him in the Sicilian villa my mother had inherited from that evil family.

The Turricci family bloodline was finished. As far as I knew. But they'd still managed to mark me forever. They'd turned me into a killer. I hadn't killed for years.

And I didn't want to return to that life.

Of course I couldn't tell her all of this right then. Maybe later. Maybe I thought it would help her to know. My focus right then was getting her away from the cliff's edge.

"Come on, Hannah." I said. She was still staring out at the sea.

I stared at her profile as she stared out at the sea. Tears streamed down her face. I took that as a good sign.

"Let's talk about this over a glass of wine. We can get in my car and drive far away. We'll find a chalet up in the Alps and make a plan...figure out how to handle this. Come up with a solution." I wasn't lying. Right then, I would have done anything, promised anything, to get her away from that cliff's edge. She acted as if she didn't hear me.

"Hannah...?"

Then she was gone. She simply stepped off the edge. The last thing I saw was a wisp of her hair floating in the air. She fell silently. She stepped off the cliff to meet her death without even a sigh or whimper. I walked slowly over to the edge, dreading what I knew I would see.

Hannah's body was crumpled on the rocks below, a pile of clothes. A slash of dark hair.

I closed my eyes to stop the tears, but they managed to squeak out anyway.

I sat on the rocks with my legs dangling off the edge for a long time before I could force my fingers to dial the numbers on my cell phone. I sat staring at the sun shining down on the sea. It was a view I had taken in so many times before from so many other shores. It was a constant in my life. It didn't matter if I was filled with joy or sorrow, the sun was there to remind me that I was alive, experiencing life and all its ups and downs. It was something. And I clung to that. My life wasn't always easy. But I was alive. And the miracle and beauty of that was something I would never take for granted. It meant that there would be pain and sorrow, but also moments of joy and beauty. Living life fully meant experiencing all the contrasts that came with it. I was willing to experience the whole package. I had no choice.

17

Ryder was the first to arrive. Again. The authorities were right behind him.

It made me wonder if he waited a few minutes each time I called him before he called the police just to make sure he got to me first. I sort of suspected he did.

And I was grateful for it.

He ran over and wrapped me in his arms.

I was surprised.

Not only that he did it but that I liked it. I folded myself into his arms.

I hadn't thought I was upset or in need of comfort until he held me. But I sank deeper into his embrace and buried my face into the soft fabric of his warm, black shirt.

"You okay?" he said, breathing the words into my hair.

I nodded my head.

Then I pulled back and looked up into his eyes. "She was just a kid."

"A messed-up kid."

All three of them were just kids. They were only a few years younger than me, true, but they seemed like babies compared to me after the life I'd lived.

We both jumped when a man cleared his throat.

Commissaire Boucher.

"I tried to stop her from jumping. She was distraught over her friend's deaths." I met his eyes, daring him to dispute my account.

He didn't answer. We locked eyes for a solid thirty seconds before he nodded.

"I'm sure you did everything you could to stop her."

I blinked back tears. I hadn't expected his sympathy.

"Can you come into the station to give an official account?"

"Of course," I said.

"We need to wrap things up here so maybe in an hour?"

"I'll meet you there," I said and turned to walk away.

Ryder followed me to the Jeep. "Why don't I drive you back? We'll get one of Boucher's men to drive the Jeep back to the villa."

I was about to refuse, but I realized my legs were weak, and my hands were trembling. I hadn't eaten or slept. Sitting back in a passenger seat sounded heavenly. Without speaking, I handed him the keys to the Jeep, pivoted and went to the passenger door of his car, yanking it open and plopping into the seat.

He laughed and got into the driver's seat.

RYDER DROPPED me off at the villa four hours later. The Jeep was in the driveway.

It had taken longer at the police station than anyone had expected. Apparently, the detective had been delayed with business at the American Embassy. With three American deaths in less than a week, it hadn't been good for the tourist business either. Reporters were swarming the police department when we arrived. Ryder took me around the back and a garage door opened for us to pull inside.

My official account was recorded.

Then Boucher told me something that surprised me. They had never taken Owen into custody.

He was never really a suspect. "He actually had an alibi," Boucher said. "He has a girlfriend in the States who he was Facetiming with on the nights of the murders. She reached out to us on his behalf. Her roommate confirmed the conversation. He apparently would sneak out of his room with Amanda and spend the time downstairs on his phone talking to his girlfriend."

"Nice guy."

Boucher gave me a look.

"We decided not to share that he had an alibi in the hopes it would flush out the real killer," he said. "We put him on a flight back to America this morning."

"Did you 'flush out' the real killer?" I asked.

Boucher ignored me and started to type on his computer.

But before I walked out, he said, "The bodies are being returned on a plane tomorrow."

"I'll be there," I said without turning around.

Later, sitting in Ryder's car in the driveway of the villa, the massive stone structure looked cold and empty and foreboding. I froze, my hand on the door handle, peering up at the dark building.

"Do you want to stay at my place tonight?" Ryder asked.

"Yes." I didn't hesitate.

He started the engine again and peeled out, kicking up dirt.

"I'll come get your things tomorrow," he said. "I should have anything you'll need for tonight."

I liked that he was making all the decisions for me. I wasn't usually that kind of a woman. I liked being in charge. But I was exhausted. For once in my life, I wanted to be taken care of. It felt nice to let down my guard and just turn off my brain.

I rolled down the window, leaned back into the passenger seat and closed my eyes, letting the cool night air caress my face.

18

Ryder's apartment was a few streets off the main promenade. He parked and then opened my door for me, reaching down to grab my hand and pull me out of my seat. He led me by my hand to a door set in the side of a stone wall. After unlocking it, he pushed it open and gestured for me to go inside. Stairs led straight up. At the top, they opened up to an airy, but small loft apartment with a bank of windows facing the bay.

There was a galley kitchen, a small living room, and a large bed took up most of the space.

Ryder pulled back the covers on the bed, handed me a towel and large shirt and pointed toward a bathroom.

"I'll sleep on the couch," he said.

Disappointment flooded me. But he already had his back to me.

He grabbed a blanket and pillow from the bed and headed for the couch.

I didn't bother with the bathroom. I stripped down to my underwear and bra and crawled under the covers. I heard a click. The room grew dark and I closed my eyes.

I woke the next morning to the smell of bacon and toast and

coffee. I sat up, my mouth watering. But something else over-rode the hollow pit of my stomach's grumbling. Something primal and urgent.

I stretched languidly, letting myself feel it, luxuriating in the deliciousness of the way my body felt as I took in my surroundings.

The entire apartment was filled with an ethereal golden light. In the distance, I could see the turquoise waters of the bay. The south of France was a paradise unto itself. I couldn't believe that Ryder woke every morning to this view. It seemed unreal. No wonder he lived here.

I squinted and saw Ryder, already dressed in his standard uniform of black jeans and button-down black shirt with the sleeves rolled up. He was standing at the stove holding a spatula.

I took him in.

My entire body felt electric as I looked at him. The veins in his forearms, his tight ass in those jeans, the muscles of his back...

Nothing was sexier than a man cooking. Okay. That's a lie. A father caring for his child was the sexiest thing ever. Thinking that made me think of Nico, and a pang of sadness zinged through me. But I pushed it away.

I watched him and, as quietly as I could, I slipped out of my underwear and bra. Then I grabbed the sheet, tugging it loose and wrapping it around me.

I got out of the bed and stretched, yawning loudly. Ryder turned and smiled. But when he saw me standing there in just a sheet, he quickly looked away before he spoke.

"Sorry, I was trying to be quiet. But it is ten."

"It is?" He still wouldn't look at me. He spoke over his shoulder.

"Yes."

"What time..." I was about to ask what time the bodies were being flown home. But he knew what I was getting at.

"One."

"Okay."

"We have time to eat."

"Do I have time to shower before breakfast?" My voice sounded strange in my ears. It sounded plaintive, unsure. Not very Gia-like. I wasn't sure why this man had this effect on me.

He didn't answer. He was busy at the stove. Bacon was sizzling. Eggs were frying. Toast was popping out of the stainless-steel toaster on his counter. Butter was in a dish on the counter. Coffee on the stove and he had squeezed fresh orange juice for us. My mouth watered to sip it. My stomach growled. I couldn't remember the last time I'd had food. But I wanted something else right then. I needed something else first.

"Ryder?"

I let the sheet slip off my shoulder.

When I said his name, there must have been something in my voice because he finally glanced at me. He took me in fully. I saw his eyes rake over me. My body burned from his gaze. Just like I wanted. His hand stayed frozen in mid-air, holding the spatula. I saw his Adam's apple bob.

My heart raced, and I realized I was holding my breath. I let the sheet drop where it puddled silently on the wooden floor. I stood there waiting, feeling vulnerable and suddenly insecure and uncertain.

He turned back to the stove. But he set the spatula down and turned off the burner.

When he turned back to me, I saw something in his eyes that I'd been denying I wanted to see since the first minute I met him.

He walked over to me so slowly that by the time he got there, I was a nervous wreck.

"It's been a really long time since I've been with anybody but my husband," I said.

He cupped my chin in his hand and leaned down. His mouth on mine was tentative at first and then grew more urgent. I knew immediately that waiting for this moment had been the right call.

Conner was hot and sweet, but it would not have been like this. This tenderness, this sophisticated knowledge of a woman's body? Only Ryder could know how I needed to be touched right then.

I fell into his embrace and let myself go completely, surrendering myself to someone else.

His arms wrapped around me from behind and roamed over my body. His fingers started at my mouth and then trailed down my neck, shoulders, and chest and finally stopped where I was throbbing the hardest. He pressed me against the kitchen counter from behind with his entire body. His fingers probed and brought me pleasure that I'd forgotten I could feel.

He stopped suddenly and turned me so I was facing him. His eyes met mine.

He was making sure.

Because of Nico. He knew this wasn't something I was doing lightly. That hesitation, and respect, made me certain that I was doing the right thing.

I swallowed and nodded.

Then he took my hand, and, without another word, led me to the bed.

I cried.

And Ryder held me. He wiped my tears and kissed them away and murmured soothing sounds in a language I did not know and didn't need to speak to understand.

19

RYDER PULLED UP TO THE CURB AT THE AIRPORT AND LEANED OVER to open my door.

"Aren't you coming inside?" I said.

He shook his head.

"I'll wait right here. Unless you need me."

"No, it's fine."

Inside the terminal, I stood at the large window, watching them load the three caskets onto the plane.

At first I didn't notice him. He stood slightly behind me.

It was Commissaire Boucher. He remained standing next to me as the caskets were loaded into the cargo hold.

"I can't imagine the grief of those three families waiting in America," I said, shaking my head.

"I wish I could say that it was the first time young people came to party here and didn't make it back home," he said.

I frowned thinking about that. He was right. People on vacation sometimes went crazy. Add alcohol and youth, and it was even worse.

"It's just sad."

"Very," he said.

I turned to look at him.

"When did you first know it was Hannah?"

"When Amanda was murdered," he said. "If she wouldn't have killed the second time, she might have got away with it."

"What are you telling the families?"

"We have passed the details of our investigation over to the American authorities. They have already told the families."

"Do the others know? The friends?"

He shrugged.

I thought of the night I met them in the club. They had seemed so close. As if they'd been friends forever and would remain that way forever.

But now I knew they would probably part ways and never speak again. Sabine had left a day earlier on her own. She'd said she wanted to be with her family. Conner was the only one going home on the same plane as the bodies of his friends. He would be the poor soul facing the families when he got off the plane.

The chances of them getting together again seemed slim to me. I even doubted they would ever speak to one another again.

It was like that sometimes.

20

WHEN WE GOT BACK TO RYDER'S PLACE, WE MADE LOVE AGAIN.

This time it was slower. In the daylight, we took the time to map one another's bodies thoroughly, and I found myself caught up in his eyes.

There was something there—a deep knowledge that this was not just a one-night stand.

At the same time, I knew that was impossible. I was leaving for Barcelona in the morning. I'd already bought my ticket. The care home had said that Nico was doing okay, on antibiotics for the pneumonia. But I needed to see him in person.

Saying goodbye to Ryder would be harder than I thought.

Maybe it was knowing that our lovemaking was short-lived that made it so tender and poignant—bittersweet.

Later, when I said I was starving, Ryder said he would cook for me.

I threw on a loose white linen dress and sandals, and we walked down to a farmer's market near the promenade to pick out ingredients for our dinner.

Or rather, Ryder picked them out.

"I will make you my specialty."

He stopped at a fish stand and asked for a large number of fresh anchovies. I wrinkled my nose.

"Um," I said, touching his elbow. "I was always the odd Italian girl who didn't like anchovies on her pizza."

"I am making pissaladière," he said in an indignant voice. "The main ingredient is anchovy."

"No clue what you just said."

"It is a delicious tart made from anchovies, onions, tomatoes and olives."

"Hmm."

"It is my specialty."

"Your only one?" I said.

"That or frog's legs," he said, turning and walking away.

"Fine," I said, huffing after him. "I'll give it a shot."

When I caught up to him, he was buying garlic, onion, tomatoes, olives, basil, pecorino cheese, and white beans.

"This all looks good," I said as sort of a peace offering.

"We will also have soupe au pistou—it's like a pesto soup. It's a little early to make it. It's more in season in July, but we will have to make do."

"Yes, we will," I said solemnly, mimicking his serious tone. He'd become French after all these years. The French were such serious fucking snobs about food. It was absurd.

Then we crossed the street and entered a bakery. I closed my eyes and inhaled.

"Now, this is heaven," I said.

"We will get fougasse," he said. "I warn you. This also has anchovies. It is superb."

"Might as well go all in, I say," I said and winked at him.

The flatbread the woman behind the counter handed him looked amazing. It had olives and cheese on top.

"Can we please go home now and eat," I said. "I'm dying over here."

He laughed and threw his arm around me. I tucked my head into his shoulder and wasn't surprised at how easily it fit there and how damn comforting it felt.

So, of course, I immediately drew back.

I was a lone wolf. I reminded myself that even if Nico weren't still in the picture, which in many ways he still was, I had vowed to never care about anyone again.

Ryder was fine. Fun. Amazing in bed. Easy company. But that was it.

For what it was worth.

A day or two of fun.

But that was it.

Thank God I was leaving in the morning.

Of course, it wasn't that easy.

After an amazing meal, that somehow made anchovies my new favorite thing, we had crazy, wild sex again.

With moonlight streaming through the windows into the darkened loft, he leaned on one elbow and took a lock of my hair between his fingers.

"You are so mysterious."

"Am not."

"Every time I think maybe I am getting to see the real Gia, you draw back."

I didn't answer. What could I say? "I'm leaving in the morning. We'll never see each other again, and I'm glad?"

But I owed him a little more than that. After all, he'd opened up about his wife and her death.

So I told him even more about Nico.

How we'd spent the past decade together. How we raised Rose. How our life wasn't easy to begin with.

I told him how I'd left the life of a killer far behind. I told him how Nico and Rose and I had settled into a normal, domestic life in Barcelona, something that I treasured deeply and had never dreamed possible.

I told him, too, how Alzheimer's had stolen our golden years away from us. Our rather his, since he was so much older than me.

I told him how Nico had pneumonia and how that was dangerous and scary and was breaking my heart.

"He is the love of my life," I said.

"Aha," Ryder said, sitting up in bed, his back against the headboard. "You are blessed to have that."

"I know I'll never have that again," I said.

He was quiet for a moment and then he said, "If you have decided it, then it will be so."

His words made me angry.

"It's not my choice," I said.

"Really?"

"It's my destiny. I'm tired of fighting against it. What you don't know—what I haven't even touched on—is that everyone I've ever loved has been taken from me one way or another. My parents were murdered. My first true love was murdered. Now, I'm losing Nico..."

"If you have decided it, then it will be so."

His repetition of those words sent fury coursing through me. I was about to leap out of bed, but he beat me to it.

I heard the shower start up in the bathroom. I sat there in bed, stewing. Furious.

He was gone for a long, long time.

I fell asleep before he returned to the bed.

21

Despite our argument the night before, I leaned over and kissed Ryder awake. He opened one eye and smiled at me.

"*Bellissima*," he said.

"You speak Italian, too?"

"A little."

I got up and made him coffee and toast with jam.

"Thank you for letting me stay here. Thank you for being there for me."

"It was my pleasure," he said.

Then I showered and dressed and was at the door.

He looked at me for a long time as I stood in the doorway.

"I called a car. It's here. I have to go."

"I wish you'd stay," he said finally.

"I have to go to him."

"I know."

While I was sitting in the back seat of the car I'd hired, my phone rang. My heart leapt into my throat. Somehow, I knew it was about Nico.

And the news was as terrible as my worst fears.

Nico was dead.

22

BEFORE I STEPPED OFF THE PLANE, I TOOK OUT MY COMPACT mirror to check my makeup. I'd spent the entire flight crying behind my dark glasses. By that point, my makeup had washed away. Now my eyes were bloodshot and puffy.

When I saw Dante standing there on the tarmac waiting for me, fresh tears pricked my eyes. I was so lucky to have him for a best friend.

I walked over to him, and he wrapped me in a hug.

I melted into his embrace. He kissed both my cheeks and then we drew away from one another.

"I'm so, so sorry."

I sniffed and nodded.

I wiped my nose on my sleeve. Like a little kid.

He gave me a look full of sorrow.

"Did you get ahold of Rose?"

I shook my head. She wasn't answering my calls, and her voice mail said it was full.

Nico had made preparations years before, as soon as he found out he had Alzheimer's. His wishes were to be cremated. He'd picked out a plot in the Barcelona cemetery.

Dante took me straight to the memory care home. Of course, they'd already removed his body. I wouldn't be able to see it. In fact, I would be picking up his ashes the next morning.

I asked to be alone as I packed up his things. I stared at his empty bed for so long that my eyes glazed over. Then I found myself crawling into the bed, burying my face in the pillow. It still smelled like him—of the soap and shampoo he'd always used and his own Nico smell. I don't know how long I lay there, but I must've fallen asleep because when I next realized it, the light had changed and someone had come in and pulled the quilt up over me. Photographs on the dresser of me and him and Rose. I'd hoped that they would help him remember us to the end, but that was too much to hope for...

I stacked the items that I would keep on the bed and filled another bag with items to donate. The items I would keep included his watch, which I would give to Rose, the photos, maybe a clothing item or two, and that was it. So little remained of such a full life.

I pulled one of his button up shirts off a hanger in the closet and held it to my nose. It didn't smell like him. It smelled like fresh laundry detergent. But it was still a favorite shirt. I flashed back to him wearing it out to dinner once. He'd looked so handsome and his dazzling grin was white against his dark skin and this white linen shirt. I held it between my fingers and remembered how we'd sat at a café table outside the restaurant. The air had been warm and the night filled with stars. We could hear the waves lapping the shore not far away. We'd shared a bottle of red wine and a huge platter of paella. We'd talked about everything and nothing at all—the latest art exhibit, what we thought of the movie we'd just seen, how we would have to agree to disagree on the latest book I'd read at his suggestion. And Rose. We always talked about Rose and how proud of her we were. She was out with her friends that night. After the waiter had cleared our plates, we'd ordered espresso and sat back in our chairs, smiling at one another.

"This moment, this magical night, is one I shall never forget," Nico said, his eyes narrowed and locked on me.

Remembering his words, a sob rose in my throat.

I knew that if Nico had even the slightest choice in the matter, he would have kept his word.

The heartbreaking thing was that he, like everyone who gets this cruel disease, doesn't get a choice.

I grabbed the tote bag and then, at the last second, I pulled the pillow that still smelled like Nico off of his bed and tucked it under my arm. I walked out without another glance.

23

We were sitting on the balcony of the Gothic Quarter apartment. I was clutching Nico's pillow in my lap. I hadn't been able to set it down since I'd plucked it off his bed.

Dante had looked at it once but never said a word.

"You going to keep this place?" he asked.

"It's not mine to keep," I said. It belonged to Rose. Wherever she was in the world. I still hadn't been able to reach her. I'd tried waking in the middle of night to call her and that hadn't worked either. I couldn't help but think she was avoiding my calls. Eva, an expert hacker, said it looked like Rose had turned off her phone.

Then she'd asked a question I hadn't wanted to face. "Is there any chance she's just avoiding you?"

"I don't know," I answered honestly. What I didn't say was that I was worried sick. I didn't need to. Eva knew. But Rose was an adult now. I couldn't rein her in. She was on a mission to hunt down and kill the Sultan. To me, who had only heard the stories, the Sultan was an ominous cult leader with strange powers I didn't even want to admit existed in this world. Rose had almost become his victim. And when he had her boyfriend, Timothy, murdered, Rose had dedicated her life to hunting down and destroying him. The final push was when she realized that Nico no longer had any idea who she was. After that, she was gone. A young woman intent on one thing—murder.

There was no room in her life for anything else. No room for love, that's for sure. It broke my heart.

"Will you stay here until you reach Rose?" Dante asked.

I shook my head. "It hurts too much to be here," I said and stood up. "In fact, I feel like I can't breathe. Can we go out? Maybe walk? Or go to the beach?"

What I really wanted to do was get on an airplane—or get in my car and drive away from all the dark shadows haunting me in Barcelona. I could feel them hovering just over my shoulders, and when I turned to look, they would disappear.

"Yeah," Dante said, trying to hide his surprise. "Let's go."

As we walked, I turned to him.

"I'm going to leave in the morning. I think I'm going to go to Indonesia. That was the last place Rose was on the grid. Eva tracked her that far, and then she disappeared. I need to find her and let her know about Nico."

"Okay," he said. "But Indonesia doesn't really narrow it down much does it?"

"I have to at least try," I said. "I have a huge favor to ask. Will you lock up the apartment for me until Rose returns? I thought I could close it up, but I can't deal with it. In fact, I'm going to a hotel tonight."

"Of course, Gia," Dante said. "Whatever you need me to do."

After stopping and buying a bottle of wine and two ceramic mugs at another shop, we headed toward the beach.

We ended up plopping down on an empty strip and drinking the wine as the sun touched the horizon. I stretched my legs out in front of me, burying my feet in the warm sand.

Dante let out a low whistle and admired my legs.

"You've got a killer tan, G."

"Got to keep up with my bestie." Dante always had me beat for the best tan each summer.

"I didn't get a chance to ask," he said. "How was Cannes?"

"It was okay."

"Just okay." I didn't feel like elaborating. It felt like a lifetime ago already.

"Did you like my friend Ryder?"

I gave a small smile. "Yeah. He's a good guy."

"Good guy?" Dante scoffed. "He's hot."

I laughed. And then, after sneaking a glance to watch his reaction, I asked, "Have you talked to him lately?"

Dante shook his head. "Not for a few weeks. When you first got there, he texted to tell me you'd landed and were safe."

"Oh."

"Why?"

"No reason."

I'd been pretty sure Ryder would keep our secrets, and I was right.

We sat there until the sun set and the wind picked up.

A chill ran across my bare legs, and I shivered.

"You okay?"

I stood and nodded.

"Good, because I'm worried about you."

"You don't need to worry," I said. "But I'm leaving here, Dante. And I'm not sure I'll ever come back."

As we walked back toward the apartment in the Gothic Quarter, I felt a peace come over me, and I knew that leaving was the right decision. I rested my head on Dante's shoulder as we walked. He looped his arm around my waist. He was the best friend I could ask for. He'd left his husband, Wayne, behind in San Diego to come be with me. He always upended his life when I needed him. I was incredibly blessed to have him in my life. He was the one person who had remained constant since I was a child.

I would lay down and die if anything happened to Dante.

"I'm flying back to San Diego tomorrow afternoon after I close up the apartment," he said as if following the train of my thoughts.

"Good. I'm sure Wayne misses you."

"He's been super busy at work, but I'm sure he does miss me," Dante said with a small laugh.

I smiled. I could not be happier that Dante and Wayne had found one another. They were good for one another.

At the door to the apartment, I paused. "I'm just going to run up and grab my bag. Will you wait here for me and walk me to my hotel when I come back down?"

"Of course."

I raced up the familiar stairs and unlocked the door. The apartment was lit with dozens of the fake wax candles that were set to come on at dusk every night. It had a cozy ambiance and held so many bittersweet memories. Slowly, I walked from room to room saying my goodbyes. I began with the most difficult room—the bedroom I'd shared with Nico for so many years. I gave myself a few minutes in each room, knowing that Dante would understand and wait all night if necessary. After visiting each room and saying a silent goodbye, I ended up in front of the altar in the small alcove by the door. I reached my hand up to touch the faces in the photos of those I had loved with all of my being. For a half second I considered scooping the contents of the altar into the bag hanging on my shoulder, but I realized that this altar needed to remain here, where it was. After I kissed my fingers and put them on the faces of those I'd loved, I tucked Nico's pillow under my arm and gently closed the door of the apartment where I'd lived my best life.

That's when I noticed that the dark shadows that had been

fluttering in my peripheral vision for the past few years were gone. Instead, I felt a lightness around me. A peace. A gratefulness I'd never felt before.

In my mind, Barcelona would be the city of my soul. It was where I lived a life I'd only dreamed could be possible.

For me, Barcelona would always be sacred. It would remain the place where, for the first and probably last time as an adult, I was able to carve out a normal life—a beautiful, soulful, gut-wrenching, but fully-lived life.

EPILOGUE

This was what I needed.

I hadn't realized it until I stepped off the plane in Padang in West Sumatra.

We'd had a layover in Kuala Lumpur but I wanted to wait to eat until I got to Padang because it was famous for its food.

I strode through the crowded marketplace, inhaling the exotic scents, my stomach growling.

Stopping at one stand I ordered a Satay Kacang, basically beef on a stick smothered in peanut sauce, and walked, chewing on that, while I perused the other stands and picked out small food items to carry on the ferry later.

As I walked, voices filtered past in several languages including ones I could easily recognize—English, Spanish, and French.

It was easy to weave through the crowd. I was traveling light.

All of my worldly possessions were in the leather backpack I had slung on one shoulder. I'd left everything behind in Barcelona at the last minute, including Nico's pillow.

The backpack contained a few changes of clothes. I had decided to adopt a uniform for my travels.

I was wearing charcoal gray cargo pants, a black tank top, and steel-toed military boots with a custom heel that held a nice-sized dagger. In my backpack, I had two more pairs of the cargo pants, five more matching tanks, a pair of gray cargo shorts, a black military-issue sweater, sandals and a fold-up rain poncho. With that capsule wardrobe, I could account for varying terrain, temperature, and weather.

I felt lighter than I had in years.

But it wasn't just the backpack.

Although my heart was still heavy with the loss of Nico, the dark shadows of dread that had been lying in wait since he first showed signs of Alzheimer's had left me.

Now, I was on a mission.

Find Rose.

I'd had a dream on the plane.

I knew that she was calling out to me across space and time.

Even if she wasn't answering her phone, it still pinged in a village on an island not far from here.

I was going to take the ferry there and then hire a driver and have them take me to the surf camp up the coast where locals and foreigners went to live simply and surf all day.

That's where Eva had last traced Rose's phone. Just last week.

I knew deep in my gut that Rose needed me.

And even if she didn't, I couldn't rest until I told her about Nico.

I knew that it would break her heart.

He was her only living relative left.

I knew how that felt.

Until Eva appeared, I'd thought I was all alone in the world, as well.

I needed to find Rose and tell her—she would never be alone as long as I walked this earth.

The story continues in *Dark Vengeance*, the next Gia Santella Thriller. Head to the next page for a sneak peek or scan the QR code below to order today!

Stay up to date with Kristi Belcamino's new releases by scanning the QR code below!
(You'll receive a **free** copy of *First Vengeance: A Gia Santella Prequel!)*

Did you enjoy *Dark Shadows?* Scan the QR code below to let us know your thoughts!

DARK VENGEANCE CHAPTER ONE

When Nico and I first looked at apartments in Barcelona, we didn't have strong ideas about what we wanted other than it be located in the Gothic Quarter. The quarter was central to everything. It was near the beach and the main pedestrian artery of the city, Las Ramblas, and it overflowed with character. Below our balcony, the narrow street was filled with small mom-and-pop shops that had everything we could possibly desire—cheese, wine, bread. You know, the basic necessities.

But when we walked into this apartment, besides its gorgeous architecture, what I fell in love with was the alcove that was specifically designated as an ofrenda—a home altar for those you loved who had died. Even though I'm Italian and it's a Mexican tradition, it spoke to me on the deepest level of my soul.

Although some people only set up ofrendas around Dia de los Muertos, mine was in place all year long.

Now, as I wheeled my gunmetal gray suitcase over to the front door, I glanced at the altar. I would miss it the most. I wasn't sure when I'd be back in Barcelona. If ever.

The ofrenda was set in a deep oval alcove in the wall that contained photos, candles, and mementos from those I'd loved the most in this life: my parents, Bobby—my first true love, and Nico—my last true love.

Nico wasn't dead, but his picture was there along with all the other people I'd loved and lost in my life.

Was that sacrilegious? Fuck if I knew.

But the truth was the Nico I'd known and loved was dead.

Alzheimer's had taken him from me. He didn't know me anymore. Now, I was just some girl he groped when I showed up. At first it had broken my heart. But once I realized that the Nico I'd known and loved was no longer there, in some ways it'd been easier to let go.

I stared at the photos. The photo of my parents was one of them smiling on a boat, their hair windblown. My mother held a glass of wine. My father had his arm around her.

I missed my parents so much. I'd been robbed of them before I was barely old enough to drink. They had been my whole world.

The photo of Bobby was a snapshot I'd taken of him in Italy. He'd been standing on our balcony looking out at the sea. He was so damn handsome. That was the day I'd finally told him I loved him. Within 24 hours he'd be dead. The son of my parents' killer took him away.

A tear slipped down my cheek as I looked at the photo of Nico.

He looked like a sophisticated movie star and a powerful leader. Which is what he had been. My greatest love. The man I had intended to spend the rest of my life with. That man had loved me more than any woman could dream of being loved, but he had been taken away from me slowly and cruelly by the creeping dementia that stole his memories and light.

When I realized that Nico was gone, I decided to never allow myself to fall in love again.

It hurt too much. Why would I fucking torture myself like that again? Who in their right mind would do that? Um...nobody.

I was fucking done.

There is an old Italian saying that we only truly love three people in our lives.

I've loved my three.

Bobby. Nico. James.

Dear, sweet James who, thank God, was still alive and thriving in San Francisco. That man had stolen my heart but then broke it into a million pieces. Because I'm a killer and he was a cop. Our relationship never stood a chance.

I reached into my bag and took out my worn metal Zippo lighter and lit the candles on my ofrenda one last time.

I lit four of them. Along with the photos and candles, I'd placed mementos that reminded me of them or items that they had loved in life.

In front of Nico's picture, I'd placed a CD of his favorite music and a bottle of tequila.

For Bobby, a bottle of the hot sauce he loved and his favorite book of poetry.

For my parents, the cigars my dad liked and the perfume my mom wore.

My phone vibrated in my bag, startling me out of my memories.

I rummaged around and found it just as the call ended. Dante.

I called him back. "Yo."

"I've been buzzing. I'm downstairs."

"Oh, fuck. The ringer is still broken. I'll buzz you in."

I hit the button and headed back to the bedroom to finish packing my second suitcase.

Soon Dante was at my side.

"Have you decided where you're going?" he said in his perfectly enunciated speech as he walked in.

I glanced up at him and was once again astonished by his good looks. The guy never aged. We'd been friends since we were kids, and he just kept getting better looking. His brilliant white smile always stood out against his burnished olive skin, and I loved how he was wearing his silky black hair a little bit long in the back nowadays at the request of his husband, Wayne. Today, he was wearing a white linen shirt with the buttons undone enough for me to see his gold necklace with the Italian cornetto and hand talisman to protect against the evil eye.

"French Riviera," I said.

I continued throwing expensive silk lingerie into my smaller suitcase. Dante had made me buy it during our last shopping spree in Paris. I would never have spent $250 on underwear otherwise, but I had to admit it made my ass look spectacular.

"Sounds fabulous," Dante said, stepping into my closet. "Why there?"

"I have no memories there."

"What? That hurts. Me. You. St. Tropez?" he started humming some song about St. Tropez and dancing around.

"I'm not going there."

"Where to, then?"

I didn't answer, but I looked pointedly at a framed poster in the hallway. It was a still from the movie *La Piscine*. The movie was set in Italy. But from the look on Dante's face, I knew he made the connection. Cannes was the film epicenter of Southern France, and the festival was next week.

"Oh. My. God."

I hid my smile.

"What will you wear?"

"I'm going to sunbathe and read and listen to music and maybe find some hot boy to fuck."

Dante stopped dancing.

I could feel his disapproval without looking at him.

"You're married."

"Am I?"

He didn't answer.

I wasn't married. Not really.

How could I be? Nico didn't know who I was. He hadn't for months.

"At least let me dress you." Dante had personal buyers at all the top designers and attended the fashion shows in Paris every year. He had impeccable taste. Thank God one of us did.

"I'm bringing every bikini I own," I said. "That's really all I plan on needing."

"Darling, if you are going to be in Cannes during the Film Festival—first, how the holy hell did you find a place to stay there right now? Oh, never mind, you're Gia. But please, please tell me you'll let me dress you for the festival."

I shrugged and tossed another bikini into the suitcase on the bed.

"I wasn't planning on going to the festival."

"I'm going to get you tickets."

I didn't argue. I loved movies. Attending the festival in Cannes could fit into my hedonistic plans. "Sure. Whatever."

"Then it's a deal. Now, what should you wear? I'm not sure you have anything in this apartment?" He started thumbing through my hangers.

"I'll find something."

"I'll handle it," he said firmly. "Someone has to stop you from wearing your beat-up leather pants and 'Fuck Authority' T-shirt."

"Rosie took that shirt from me years ago."

Rosie was Nico's daughter. The closest thing I had to a child. She was off somewhere killing someone. Because, apparently, that's what the women in my family did. We couldn't help it. But there were always evil fuckers who needed to be killed.

"Will you let me do what I do best?" Dante said, in seventh heaven. Shopping and dressing me was his favorite thing ever. Or at least that's how it seemed.

"Yeah. I'll go watch some movies. And you can dress me for them."

Dante was chattering on and on about how he knew the perfect dress for me and that he might have to order it and have it sent to me in Cannes. But I would also need three other ones and...blah blah blah. I let him ramble. It made him happy so I tolerated it. And the simple fact was that I looked like shit when I dressed myself.

Attending the Cannes Film Festival was probably a legit reason to dress up.

Dante frowned. "There is nothing here. Nothing at all. Come with me," he said and grabbed my hand. "There is one place in town—one place in all of Barcelona—that might possibly have a dress that will do in a pinch if I can't get the dresses I have in mind ordered in time."

I couldn't help but laugh. God love Dante.

I grabbed my bag and followed him out the door, giving one last glance at the candles burning on the altar. I usually was very careful about blowing them out before I left the apartment, but I was feeling careless, reckless, and a small part of me thought that burning the place down would be apropos—leaving the charred remains of my life behind. But then I remembered other people lived in the building and leaned over to blow them out.

Then I steeled myself for some hard-core shopping. I wished I had some marijuana but would have to shop stone-cold sober.

But if I was being honest with myself, I was happy to spend another few hours with Dante.

He had flown into Barcelona from San Diego when he heard I was taking off for a few months...or forever.

It would be strange to leave Nico behind and not visit him daily while hoping there might be a glimmer of recognition in his eyes when he saw me.

There never was.

Nico was in good hands. I paid a small fortune every month for the memory care center to treat him like a king. It took about six months of him not recognizing me for me to realize my daily, doting presence there was no longer for him, only for me. And that it hurt like hell to be around him.

I was a coward.

I was going to leave him. Maybe forever.

If I thought there was the slightest, smallest part of him that still remembered me, I would stay. But there wasn't.

My heart was shattered.

Every morning I woke and lay in bed waiting for the dark shadows to recede from my nightmares only to realize that it wasn't a bad dream. It was my life.

Finally, I realized I had to leave Barcelona. At first I wanted to buy a house in the mountains somewhere and live like a recluse. There was still a chance I might. But right then, all my body craved was sunshine.

I'd spent the past few years as a caregiver, taking care of Nico, trying to glimpse fragments of who he used to be before he became angry and confused.

We rarely stepped outside unless it was to take him out to the garden for a walk. But now he refused to do even that.

I needed to lay in the sun and do things that weren't good for me so I didn't have to feel or think anymore.

Cannes would be the backdrop for my debauchery.

And I was happy to play it out there with all the other privileged fuckers who had everything that money could buy and yet wandered around hungrily trying to fill the empty void in their souls by spending recklessly, drinking too much, fucking everything with a heartbeat, and taking massive amounts of drugs.

DARK VENGEANCE CHAPTER TWO

Nico was slouched in his leather lounger watching TV when I walked into his room.

He looked up at me, and for the smallest fraction of a second there seemed to be a glimmer of recognition in his eyes. Then he gave a wolfish smile.

"You my new nurse?"

I played along. "Do you want me to be?"

He shrugged. "I've seen worse."

I laughed out loud. It was that or cry.

He laughed too. But then he said, "I'm just giving you a hard time. You are a beautiful woman. When I was much younger I would've pursued you with everything I had."

I blinked back my tears. "I bet you were something else."

"Oh, boy, was I," he said and frowned. "At least that's what I've been told."

Even having a picture of me hugging him on the dresser in his room wasn't enough to jog his memory of our life together. He might look at it for a few seconds but would then ask why and where we had taken it.

But as hard as it was for me, Rose couldn't handle it at all.

She'd taken every picture of us as a family and herself out of his room.

I don't even know if she still came to visit him. She wouldn't answer when I asked.

She was in a dark place, and I couldn't reach her.

I called her on my way over to tell her I was leaving Barcelona for a while.

She didn't answer her phone so I left a message. Typical.

"What's on the agenda today?" Nico said, standing. I tried not to notice him reach out to grip the arm of the chair to steady himself. He was frowning.

"I thought we would take a walk in the garden," I said. "Get a little fresh air and sunshine."

"That's what you all say."

"That's because it's good for you."

He shuffled over to me. Along with the decline in his mental health, he had grown frail over the past few years. It was just another knife in my heart.

I wanted to help him, but I knew his ego couldn't handle it.

Outside, we walked for a while and then sat on a bench near a row of flowers.

He looked over at me., wringing his hands. At first it had bothered me, but the nurses told me it was common with Alzheimer's patients, and I'd gotten used to it. It was, like everything about Nico now, including the colostomy bag, so unlike the man I'd loved for so long.

"Do I know you?" he asked.

I smiled. "Yes."

"I mean before this?"

"What do you think?"

He stared at me hard. "I get really confused sometimes."

"It's okay," I said in the most comforting voice I could. Sometimes when I was with him and he was confused, he would grow angry and violent. It scared me. But I also didn't blame him. I was pissed off too.

Then he shook his head. He turned and stared straight ahead and said, "Maybe in another life."

"I think you're right. In another life."

"Do you believe in that?" he asked.

"Of course. Don't you?"

I'd never seen anything in my life as beautiful as his smile just then. "Yes. Yes, I do."

I looked away so he wouldn't see the tears falling down my cheeks.

Suddenly, he stood.

"I'm tired, nurse," he said. "I'm sorry I don't remember your name. I forget most things."

"I never told you my name. It's Gia."

He nodded. "That's a nice name."

"Thank you."

"Can you show me back to my room? I think I should take a nap."

"I'd be happy to do that, Mr. Morales."

I used his real name to see if he reacted. He didn't.

After I tucked him into bed and pulled the curtains in his room, I gave him a kiss on the cheek as I said goodbye. He acted surprised by the kiss, his forehead wrinkling up and his eyes squinting.

Of course he did.

But then he immediately seemed to forget it.

"Sleep well, Mr. Morales."

He didn't answer.

As I walked outside to the waiting car, I wondered if it was the last time I was going to see the man I'd considered my husband for so many years.

ALSO BY KRISTI BELCAMINO

Enjoying Kristi Belcamino? Scan the code below to see her Amazon Author page!

Gia Santella Crime Thriller Series

Vendetta

Vigilante

Vengeance

Black Widow

Day of the Dead

Border Line

Night Fall

Stone Cold

Cold as Death

Cold Blooded

Dark Shadows

Dark Vengeance

Dark Justice

Deadly Justice

Deadly Lies

Additional books in series:

Taste of Vengeance

Lone Raven

Vigilante Crime Series

Blood & Roses

Blood & Fire

Blood & Bone

Blood & Tears

Queen of Spades Thrillers

Queen of Spades

The One-Eyed Jack

The Suicide King

The Ace of Clubs

The Joker

The Wild Card

High Stakes

Poker Face

Standalone Novels

Coming For You

Sanctuary City

The Girl in the River

Buried Secrets

Dead Wrong (Young Adult Mystery)

Gabriella Giovanni Mystery Series

Blessed are the Dead

Blessed are the Meek

Blessed are Those Who Weep

Blessed are Those Who Mourn

Blessed are the Peacemakers

Blessed are the Merciful

Nonfiction

Letters from a Serial Killer

ALSO BY WITHOUT WARRANT

More Thriller Series from Without Warrant Authors

Dana Gray Mysteries by C.J. Cross

Girl Left Behind

Girl on the Hill

Girl in the Grave

The Kenzie Gilmore Series by Biba Pearce

Afterburn

Dead Heat

Heatwave

Burnout

Deep Heat

Fever Pitch

Storm Surge (Coming Soon)

Willow Grace FBI Thrillers by Anya Mora

Shadow of Grace

Condition of Grace (Coming Soon)

Gia Santella Crime Thriller Series

by Kristi Belcamino

Vendetta

Vigilante

Vengeance

Black Widow

Day of the Dead

Border Line

Night Fall

Stone Cold

Cold as Death

Cold Blooded

Dark Shadows

Dark Vengeance

Dark Justice

Deadly Justice

Deadly Lies

Vigilante Crime Series by Kristi Belcamino

Blood & Roses

Blood & Fire

Blood & Bone

Blood & Tears

Queen of Spades Thrillers by Kristi Belcamino

Queen of Spades

The One-Eyed Jack

The Suicide King

The Ace of Clubs

The Joker

The Wild Card

High Stakes

Poker Face

AUTHOR'S NOTE

When I was 16, I read Jackie Collins' book, *Lucky*, and it rocked my world. For the first time in my prolific reading life (yes, I was the kid holed up in my room reading as many books as I could as often as I could), I met a character who was not only Italian-American like me, but a strong, powerful, and successful badass woman who didn't take crap from anybody and loved to have sex!

Although I had dreamed of being a writer, it never seemed like a realistic dream and my attempts at writing seemed pitiful. So I studied journalism and became a reporter—it was a way to be a writer and have a steady paycheck.

It was only when I was in my forties that I got the guts to write a book. And it was a few years after that I was brave enough to write the character I really wanted to write—Gia Santella.

She's not Lucky Santangelo, of course. I mean, nobody could be as cool as Lucky is, but I like to think that maybe Gia and Lucky would have been friends.

Gia is my alter ego. The woman who does and says things I

never could or would, but whom I admire and would love to be friends with.

If you like her, I'm pretty sure we'd be the best of friends in real life!

x Kristi

ABOUT THE AUTHOR

Kristi Belcamino is a USA Today bestseller, an Agatha, Anthony, Barry & Macavity finalist, and an Italian Mama who bakes a tasty biscotti.

Her books feature strong, kickass, independent women facing unspeakable evil in order to seek justice for those unable to do so themselves.

In her former life, as an award-winning crime reporter at newspapers in California, she flew over Big Sur in an FA-18 jet with the Blue Angels, raced a Dodge Viper at Laguna Seca, attended barbecues at the morgue, and conversed with serial killers.

During her decade covering crime, Belcamino wrote and reported about many high-profile cases including the Laci Peterson murder and Chandra Levy disappearance. She has appeared on *Inside Edition* and local television shows. She now writes fiction and works part-time as a reporter covering the police beat for the St. Paul *Pioneer Press*.

Her work has appeared in such prominent publications as *Salon*, the *Miami Herald*, *San Jose Mercury News*, and *Chicago Tribune*.

facebook.com/kristibelcaminowriter
instagram.com/kristibelcaminobooks
tiktok.com/@kristibelcaminobooks

Printed in the USA
CPSIA information can be obtained
at www.ICGtesting.com
CBHW071141270224
4725CB00009B/334